THE LIFE AND TIMES OF ERNIE O'NEIL

Colin D. MacDonald

First published 1999
Copyright © 1999 Colin D. MacDonald

The author asserts their moral rights in the work

This book is copyright. Except for the purposes of fair reviewing,
no part of this publication may be reproduced or transmitted in
any form or by any means, electronic or mechanical, including
photocopying, recording, or any information storage and retrieval system,
without permission in writing from the publisher.
Infringers of copyright render themselves liable to prosecution.

ISBN 0-909051-13-5

Published by Certes Press
P.O. Box 2151, Christchurch, New Zealand
Production and design by Orca Publishing Services Ltd

Printed in Malaysia

INTRODUCTION

Those of you who have been to the West Coast will recognise it as a pretty unique sort of a place. If you haven't been there you should get over there without delay and see it for yourself.

What makes it so unique? Well, there's the mountains, the rivers and the bush. 'Okay,' you say, 'other places have these features too.' Well, what about the rugged coastline, the glaciers and the rugged people? People who still know how to enjoy themselves. People who care about their neighbours. People who know what it is to see and appreciate a beautiful sunset over the sea or the sight of a shoal of whitebait swimming upstream towards their net. Sure, they aren't as plentiful as they used to be but there's still more than you would find in other places and the trout and ducks are there in season. And where else can you live in town and be on the beach, in the bush or down at the river in about ten minutes? It's a great place for the kids: but, I wonder, do they appreciate it?

Okay, so it rains a lot. But without the rain you wouldn't have all that lovely bush, the green grass and the crystal clear water in the rivers and streams. And when you get a fine sunny day there's nowhere better.

'It's a Coast day,' they'll tell you. 'When you get a good day it *is* a good day' – and who will dispute that?

Of course, even the Garden of Eden had its disadvantages. There are no serpents on the Coast but there is a particularly pesky little critter: the sandfly. These thirsty little pests wait around picnic places until the tourists arrive and, just after they have unpacked their picnic lunch, in swoop the sandflies for a pint of fresh blood – so take some insect repellent. Of course, they will tell you it is only the little jokers that you see: the big fellers wait back in the bush for the little guys to carry the victims back to them!

If you decide to live on the Coast be prepared to become part of the scene; otherwise you may become rather lonely. There is an old saying over there that if they aren't calling you by your Christian name within a week, you might as well pack up and leave town. However, this is not a travel brochure for the West Coast but rather an introduction to a story about one of the Coast's most colourful characters.

CHAPTER ONE

Now I reckon you'll agree with me that the Coast has more than its fair share of colourful characters. But don't get me wrong, I'm not degrading the place for that. I reckon these blokes (and blokesses!) enhance the district and help to make it the unique place that we all know about. You see, that's the difference between country areas like the Coast and the big cities. These characters don't exist in the cities, or if they do you don't see them because they're swallowed up in the crowd. Besides, they don't have time to become characters; they're too busy trying to make money. On the Coast everyone from a politician to a publican, a carpenter to a cow cocky, or a truckie to a timber worker has the potential to become a colourful character. The best example of one of these characters that I ever ran into on the Coast was a little guy called Ernie O'Neil. When I first met Ernie he owned a scrubby 200 acres and a gold claim up Pegleg Creek, about ten miles from the town of Timber Creek, which, in its turn, is thirty five miles from Port Thompson, the main town.

I believe Ernie once had hair on his head just like me and you, but by the time I met him he was as bald as a Braeburn apple – what he lacked in the thatch department, however, was compensated for by the undergrowth on his chin: he had the most luxuriant crop of whiskers this side of the Ngaio Gorge. His beard was so unique that he had been debarred from entering beard-growing contests from one end of the Coast to the other for the previous two years.

In fact his whiskers were so thick that his drinking cobbers reckoned they had never seen his mouth. They suggested that he drink his beer through a straw but Ernie scoffed at that and said, 'Look youse jokers, when I can't drink me beer *then* it's time to worry. Anyway, the old whiskers are just the caper for strainin' the impurities out of the brew.'

Somewhere about where his mouth should be, the beard was stained yellow by the nicotine from his inevitable ciggy. The droopy fag was jammed into an old cigarette holder which bobbed up and down as he talked, which was something, along with beer drinking, at which Ernie excelled. One day when he was holding forth in the bar of the Golden Nugget, he struck a match and the head flew off and landed in his beard. His mate Ces grabbed the nearest glass of beer, which happened to be Ernie's, and threw it over the smouldering thicket. 'Aw cripes,' objected Ernie. 'Yer didn't 'ave to do that, mate – the old beard's fireproof'.

He always rolled his own smokes, carrying his tobacco and papers around in an old Park Drive tobacco tin. The tin was so battered it looked like the original Park Drive tin. He despised anyone who smoked tailor-mades. 'Them coffin nails are only suitable for sissies and women,' he said. He didn't approve much of women either, 'always fussin' around and wantin' yer to clean up, change yer shirt, mow the lawn an' that. A man's better off on his own, like.' Rumour had it that there was a romance over in Christchurch after the war, but the girl told him that, if he was serious, he would have to get rid of the beard: Ernie decided to keep the beard and stay single.

He was a short, stocky little joker with bandy legs. His beady little eyes looked out from beneath shaggy eyebrows. His hands were hard and calloused and looked as rough as old pine bark. The little finger of his left hand was missing: a hungry saw bench had removed it a few years before. Ernie would never have won a contest for the best-dressed man. He wore an old checked bush shirt, corduroy trousers, patched at both knees and tucked into an old pair of boots, and, if it was really wet, he wore an old oilskin and gumboots – not that he usually approved of gumboots, which was unusual for a Coaster. 'A'right for cow cockies,' he would say, 'but they are hell on yer feet and they make holes in yer socks, like' – which was a bit of a laugh really because I don't reckon he owned a pair of socks that didn't have holes in them. A battered old wet and dry hat completed his attire. Ernie only spent money on things he could eat and drink, mostly drink, if he could get away with it.

His sister, Phyllis, was always going on about his disreputable clothing. Once, when her daughter got married, she managed, after much persuasion, to get Ernie into one of her husband's suits but she had to relent on the tie as Ernie flatly refused to wear one; and anyway nobody would have seen it because of the beard. Phyllis mistakenly suggested he shave off the beard for the occasion. Ernie was horrified and threatened to boycott the wedding altogether so Phyllis said, 'Very well, but you behave yourself and don't show yourself up in front of our city friends and relations.' Very conscious of that sort of thing was Phyllis – bit like the Orientals saving face. Ernie reckoned his sister was a bit of a snob, but he was fond of her in his funny way.

The daughter was marrying the boy of Connolly from down at Port Thompson. He was a successful young lawyer and regarded by Phyllis as a 'good catch' for her daughter. Ernie, with his usual contempt for anyone in the professions, reckoned he was a bit of a ponce but Phyllis thought he was such a 'naice gentlemanly young fellow' and was always going on about how he came from such a good family. 'His father is the mayor, you know, and his mother is a Fortesque from over the hill in Christchurch,' she would say. Ernie thought it was a bit like putting the poor girl to the stud. He was all for giving her half a dozen opossum traps for a wedding present and it took quite a bit of hard talking by Phyllis and her husband Ron to persuade him otherwise. Half-way through the reception, Ernie said in a whisper, which carried right round the hall, 'I can't stick this bloody jacket,' and he threw it on the floor to reveal the old bush shirt underneath. Phyllis cried and said that he had ruined the day but Ernie laughed and said, 'Don't worry, sis. She's a good weddin'. What about one of youse waiter jokers gettin' me another beer?'

The city folks thought the whole situation hilarious and that the funny little man quite made the day.

Ernie had been born to an overworked woman on a poverty-stricken dairy farm right at the end of the Thompson River Flats Road. He was the younger of two children, his sister Phyllis being older by two years. His parents, in their wisdom, had christened him Ernest but he was known as Ernie to most from an early age.

By the time I made his acquaintance the only people who still called him Ernest were his sister Phyllis and Father O'Halloran, the parish priest, who was always trying, quite unsuccessfully, to get him to attend mass. Ernie didn't have much time for religion, reckoning that God had enough to do forgiving all the bad bastards without worrying about him. His old man, an inveterate muddler and hard task-master, worked his wife, Ernie, and Phyllis like slaves. As long as he could remember Ernie had hand-milked the cows before and after school. Weekends were spent cutting gorse, blackberry and ragwort, which grew again as fast as it was cut. Once, when he was a bit older, he suggested to the old man that he buy some weed-killer and do the job properly; that suggestion met with a cuff around the ear and a lecture on being careful with money.

Ernie was determined from an early age that cow cockying wasn't for him. His parents were very religious and the old man reckoned that hard work was good for the soul and a sure way of opening the gates of heaven. Ernie thought about that a lot and reckoned that the old man must be God's right-hand man by now. He would say, 'I'd rather stoke them fires down below – if you've got to slave yer guts out to get to heaven. Anyway, I've had a fair bit of experience stokin' them heaps of gorse and blackberry on the farm.'

Halfway through standard six he left school, much to the teacher's relief, and shot through to Nelson, where he worked at the only thing he knew anything about – milking cows. He hated it and after a few weeks told the boss what he could do with the job, the farm and everything else. His next job was fruit-picking. He was doing quite well at that too until one day while driving the tractor along the rows of trees, picking up the full boxes of apples, he accidentally caught a ladder with the corner of the trailer. Down came the ladder, picker and all. There were apples everywhere, and what made matters worse was the fact that the picker fell on to the trailer and upset most of the full boxes. The boss was far from being amused and the picker wasn't exactly happy about it either, what with a broken arm and severe bruising. His comments about Ernie and his ancestry, and what he would do to the little squirt if he ever saw him again, left Ernie in no doubt that, discretion being the better part of valour, he should leave the immediate area without delay. He said to the boss, 'I don't think I'm really cut out for this fruit-pickin' caper. I reckon I'll finish up.'

'Yer darn right yer will, yer clumsy little bastard,' replied the boss, 'Yer get off this place pronto and don't yer never come back, see?'

He worked for a short time in another orchard at Motueka and, after the season finished and with a couple of brushes with the law behind him, he got a job in a sawmill over the hill in Takaka. The big circular saws biting into the mighty rimu and totara logs fascinated him and he went through a period of contentment. World War 2 broke out and Ernie, now 18, having made a pass at the boss' daughter and received a slap in the face from her and a black eye from her old man, took off for the nearest recruiting office and enlisted in time to go overseas with the First Echelon. Always a rebel, he spent a fair bit of his time being picked up by the Military Police or being put on charge by his NCOs for insubordination. He made a good fighting soldier but had no time for officers, NCOs – or discipline. Three times he was promoted to corporal in the field but, as soon as his unit came out of the line, he got into trouble again and was busted back to private. His commanding officer wished there was a rank lower than private to which he could demote Ernie.

After a few weeks back in Maadi Base Camp, during which time he had miraculously kept out of trouble or hadn't been caught, he got leave and went into Cairo with three of his mates. As always, leave to Ernie meant finding the nearest bar and getting plastered. After walking around for a while they found a bar in a fairly seedy part of the city and the foursome settled down to some steady drinking. Their session was getting well under way when in walked six South Africans. They were of the arrogant Boer variety and started to bait the Kiwis about the All Blacks. One thing led to another and it was not long before the fists began to fly. The room was soon turned into a battleground as furniture and bottles were smashed and used as weapons. When the big mirror at the back of the bar was smashed by a flying bottle, the proprietor came out of hiding and made a dash for the street yelling for the MPs.

CHAPTER TWO

The result of all this was that Ernie was in trouble again; real serious trouble with a capital 'T'. One of the South Africans had been badly hurt and Ernie and his companions found themselves awaiting court martial and a certain prison sentence.

His platoon commander, Lt. Adams, pleaded with the CO, but to no avail. The colonel said that it was out of his hands, that he had had enough of the little bugger, and that he deserved all he got. 'With O'Neil's record, he'll get the book thrown at him and serve him right,' he said.

Before the trial could begin, the battalion got orders to go back up the line. It was a few days before the Battle of El Alamain and every able-bodied man was needed. The colonel had a word with the provost marshal, who reluctantly agreed that Ernie and his mates would be returned to their unit but would be re-arrested after the battle.

'Okay, give him back his gun,' ordered the colonel, 'and he had better hope that he is killed up there because HQ is hopping mad with the little bugger.'

Soon after the colonel's conversation with the provost marshal a burly MP corporal flung open the door of Ernie's cell.

'Okay, O'Neil,' he shouted, 'On yer feet. Stand at attention, man. Head up, shoulders back! You're going back to yer unit 'cos they want every man up the line, although what use you'll be Gawd only knows. Now don't think you're getting off scot-free because, after the battle, you'll be back in here quicker than you can remember yer old mum's name – that's if yer ever had a mum, which I doubt. Understand?'

'Yeah,' replied Ernie.

'Yeah what,' roared the corporal.

'Yeah, corporal,' said Ernie.

'That's better,' said the corporal. 'Now right turn. Double march. Left, right, left, right, left wheel.'

And so Ernie returned to the war.

His platoon commander, Lt. Adams, sent for him and said, 'Ernie, you are going back to the unit again but don't think you're out of the wood yet. When we come back they're going to put you in clink again. The colonel can't and won't do anything for you and I can't say I blame him. You're just a colossal pain in the arse, man. Now get out of here and get your gear together and be ready to move out in half an hour.'

'Yeah righto, sir.' replied Ernie, turning, leaving the tent and running into the sergeant just outside.

'G'day, serg,' he greeted cheerfully.

'What the hell are you doing here, O'Neil?' asked the sergeant.

'I'm back in the unit, that's what,' replied Ernie. 'The old Eighth Army couldn't fight a war without the boy from Timber Creek.'

'Oh Gawd,' moaned the sergeant. 'What have I done to deserve all this? Okay O'Neil, rattle yer dags and get lined up with the others: and God help yer if yer put a foot wrong 'cos I'll have yer, I promise yer.' Shortly after this the battalion boarded their trucks and, joining hundreds of others, headed out into the desert.

A few days after the initial breakthrough, Ernie was in a slit trench with Lt. Adams and two other men. The rest of the platoon was spread out in similar trenches on each flank. An Australian unit was on their immediate left and had suffered severe casualties earlier in the day from a German counter-attack. The Kiwis could see a wounded man lying caught up in barbed wire directly in front of them. He was groaning a lot and calling for water. He was safe as long as he lay flat but was unable to free himself from the wire because of his wounds. 'Poor sod,' said Lt. Adams, 'Wish we could help him, but it would be suicide to go out there – it's right in line with that Jerry machine-gun.'

'Reckon I could get there,' said Ernie. 'There's enough dead ground for a little bloke like me to crawl across. I might have to run the first few yards but, once I'm in that dead ground, I should be Jake. I could lie up with him for the rest of the day and then we could crawl back after dark. You blokes can give me coverin' fire while I get out there.'

'Cripes Ernie, it'll be pretty dicey, mate,' said the lieutenant, 'but, yeah, I guess if you are willing it's worth a go. Are you sure you want to do it, Ernie?'

'Yeah I'll go,' replied Ernie. 'At least it will save havin' to listen to him moanin' and groanin' all night. He might be a bloody Aussie but most of them are not bad blokes and, like me, they like their beer.'

'Well, I'm sure that's a good recommendation coming from you, Ernie,' laughed Lt. Adams. He called out to the riflemen and to the Bren gunner in the next trench and to put down a covering fire on his command, but to watch out for Ernie out front.

The pitiless sun beat down on the men in the trenches and the wounded Australian caught up in the wire continued to call for water. Lt. Adams wiped the sweat from his brow and said, 'I think you'd better go now, Ernie. It's not going to get any cooler for quite a while yet and we don't know how long that poor bugger will last without water. You'd better take a spare water bottle with you and have a slug of this before you go.' He passed Ernie a small flask of whisky, which Ernie proceeded to try and empty as quickly as possible.

'Hey hang on, you greedy little bugger. I meant a wee slug – not the whole blooming lot,' said the lieutenant. 'Right, away you go and be careful, mate.'

He gave the order to fire and, as the bullets from the Bren and the rifles scythed toward the German lines, Ernie scrambled out of the trench, dashed across the open ground, and flung himself down behind a low ridge, which ran diagonally across the front of the trench and ended where the wounded Australian lay. As long as Ernie lay prone he could not be seen by the Germans. Wriggling and squirming through the sand, he joined the Aussie beside the wire.

'By God, he's made it,' said Lt. Adams with a sigh of relief.

''Ow yer goin'?' asked Ernie.

'Not too good, mate,' replied the Aussie. 'Can't get me leg clear of this wire and I can't get at me bloody water bottle. Hey, you're a Kiwi.'

'Right,' answered Ernie, 'now just keep yer leg still while I cut this 'ere wire and we'll 'ave yer out of there in two shakes: 'ave to wait till dark to get yer back – but I'll see what I can do about yer leg.'

'Cripes, mate,' said the Aussie. 'Didn't think I would be in debt to a flamin' Kiwi.'

'Please yerself,' said Ernie. 'If I was in your position the devil himself could rescue me, like. Right that's got the wire cut. Now, let's 'ave a look at yer leg.'

Drawing his bayonet Ernie slit the leg of the Australian's shorts, as the wound was high up on the leg. The bullet appeared to have passed right through the fleshy part of the thigh. The wound was bleeding slowly and it looked as though the arteries had not been severed. Ernie reached round for his first aid kit and must have exposed his arm to the enemy; for a shot rang out and a bullet ripped through the cuff of his sleeve.

'Cripes, bloody close that!' he exclaimed. 'Nearly smashed me drinkin' elbow.'

'Want to be careful, mate,' said the Aussie. 'Worst thing that could happen to a man would be to bugger up his drinkin' elbow. How's the wound look?'

'Not too bad,' said Ernie. 'Bullet missed the artery. I'll just wrap a bandage round it and yer should be okay till we get yer back.'

'Good,' said the Aussie. 'Meantime, how about a drink of water? I'm drier than this bloody sand.'

'Sorry, mate,' apologised Ernie passing over his canteen, 'ere yer are, get that into yer. We'll just have to hang about here until she gets dark, then we'll see about gettin' yer back. Me name's Ernie O'Neil, from Timber Creek in New Zealand. What's yours?'

'Gee, what a coincidence! I'm Andy Miller, also from Timber Creek – but mine's in the Northern Territory. Thanks a million for coming out to get me.'

'No trouble, mate,' said Ernie. 'Do this sort of thing all the time.'

'Aw yeah. Pull the other one,' replied the Aussie. 'How long do yer reckon we'll have to wait before we can get out of here?'

'Got to wait until dark,' answered Ernie. 'Are yer all right, mate?'

'Yeah, I'll survive,' said Andy.

The two men chatted away for a couple of hours, the Aussie taking frequent swigs at the water bottle. The hot, searing sun started to sink towards the western horizon, appearing to speed up as it neared its objective. Suddenly it was gone and, as happens in the tropics, a blanket of darkness shrouded the desert. It immediately began to get cooler, giving the wounded man some relief.

'About time to go,' announced Ernie. 'Can yer drag yer leg okay, Andy?'

'Reckon so,' replied Andy. 'Be glad to get out of this.'

Under the cover of darkness the two men shuffled their way back to the slit trenches, with Ernie calling softly to his mates that all was well. They had one fright when a German flare went up, but, by lying prone until the flare had burnt out, they were able to regain the trench without further problems. On arrival Andy was put on a stretcher to be taken over to the Australian lines. Before he was taken away, he grasped Ernie's hand in a firm grip and said, 'I'll never forget what you did for me, Ernie. I hope we meet again sometime.'

'Yeah,' said Ernie. 'Maybe we could meet up and have a few beers in Cairo sometime.'

'I'm afraid it'll be a long time before you can have a few beers in Cairo again, Ernie,' pointed out Lt. Adams. 'Don't forget you go back into clink when we get out of here.'

A few days later the battalion was relieved and retired from the front.

The MPs collected Ernie and he was back in the cells again.

'There yer are, yer miserable little sod!' roared the MP corporal. 'Yer holiday's over. Now the whole 8th Army is goin' to come down on yer like a ton of bricks. Yer case comes up in three days' time. Have yer nominated an officer to defend yer? Not that it'll make much difference. The best lawyer in the world wouldn't get you off. You're for a few years' hard labour, you are.'

'Yeah, my platoon commander, Lt. Adams. He's goin' to defend me.'

'Right then, me lad,' said the corporal, 'I'll leave yer to meditate on yer sins,' and he went out, slamming the cell door behind him. The cell was very spartan to say the least. Taking up one wall was a hard wooden bed with a thin straw palliasse and a couple of worn blankets folded on top of it: a bucket in the corner completed the furnishings. A small barred window, high up in the end wall, let in some light but was far to high too allow the occupant to see out. Ernie sat on the bed and contemplated his plight. He had really balled things up this time. Having always been used to his freedom and the great outdoors, he didn't reckon he could stick prison life. Oh sure, he had been in the guardroom cell a few times but that was only for a few days at a time and the guys in charge weren't too bad. Better than these Pommy MPs anyway – real stroppy sods they were. He supposed they would be in charge of any prison to which he was sent.

'A joker like me will go flamin' mad in there,' he said to

himself. 'It would have been better if I had got killed. Why was I such a dopey prick? If I could only get out of this mess I'd behave meself until the war is over, so help me Gawd, I would.' Mind you, he had said this before but somehow always seemed to forget his promise to himself, but maybe, just maybe, this time he meant it. Bit late to think of that, though. The next morning, after he had eaten a frugal breakfast and folded up his bedding, the door flew open and an MP yelled at him, 'On yer feet and stand at attention for the officer!'

Lt. Adams walked in and, after instructing the MP to leave he said, 'At ease, Ernie. Sit down. How are you?'

'Pretty miserable, sir. I've been a right bloody fool this time. It's the worst trouble I've ever been in.'

'Yeah you're right there, Ernie. Look I've had a yarn to the colonel and, because of what you did out there rescuing that Aussie, there's a chance we may be able to get the charges dismissed. Only a chance, mind – I can't promise anything – if you hadn't been such a bloody fool and had kept your nose clean, you would have got a medal for what you did but there's no way with this charge hanging over you that you will get a gong.'

'I don't want no bloomin' medal. What I did was nothin'. We couldn't let the poor bastard suffer out there – even if he was an Aussie.'

'Ernie, what you did was the act of a very brave man.'

'If you and the colonel can get me off, sir, they can keep all their medals and I'll promise t' toe the line in future.'

'If, and I stress the word if, we can get you off, you'll have to take a pull. If you don't, the good Lord help you because I'm damn sure no one else will.'

'Gee, thanks, sir,' said Ernie with genuine gratitude showing in his eyes. 'You're a pretty good bloke for an officer.'

'Coming from you that's praise indeed,' said the lieutenant with a twinkle in his eye. 'Keep your chin up Ernie and good luck, mate. We'll be doing our best for you.'

He knocked on the door and the MP marched in.

'Stand at attention, O'Neil,' he barked.

'All right, corporal, no need for all that,' said the Lieutenant as he left.

'We don't do it quite like that in the Kiwi army, eh? Well, my friend ,we'll have much pleasure in showin' yer how we do it in the British army – specially the prison section of it. A few weeks in there and you'll wish yer hadn't been born; and you're goin' to have years of it to look forward to.' He turned about and left the cell leaving Ernie to his thoughts.

For the rest of the day and far into the night Ernie thought about his future. Would the 'brass' listen to his colonel? If they didn't his future was pretty bleak. Would he ever see New Zealand again or would he go mad in the military prison sweating it out doing hard labour? He was sure he wouldn't be able to stand very much of it.

The next day after breakfast, the pommy MP threw open the cell door and said 'On yer feet, yer little louse. You're going back to your unit. Buggered if I know how you Kiwis do it. One day you're on charge, then yer officer arrives and the next day yer free. Devil looks after his own, I reckon.'

This episode appeared to teach Ernie a real lesson: for the rest of the war he seemed to keep out of trouble, well, serious trouble anyway. He was slightly wounded in Italy and spent a few days in hospital – something he didn't like very much. Towards the end of the war he was once again promoted to corporal and he arrived back in New Zealand holding that rank.

CHAPTER THREE

After he was discharged from the army Ernie drifted about a bit, working in a variety of jobs, never lasting long at any of them. It was during this time that he decided to grow a beard and never shave again.

'The sergeant made me shave every day,' he complained. 'It's a wonder I didn't wear me face out. From now on shavin's out.' And so the famous beard was born.

At that stage in his life there was nothing to draw him back to his old home on the West Coast: his memories were mostly of hard times on the farm and his father and mother had both died while he was overseas. He reckoned that the old man and God would be busy arguing about the best way to cut and burn gorse, etc. – that's if there was any gorse in heaven. If there wasn't you could bet yer last couple of bob there'd be some other pest to take its place, or so Ernie reckoned anyway.

After the bank and stock firm took their share of the proceeds from the sale of the farm, there was virtually nothing left for Ernie and his sister Phyllis. She had married Ron Bassett, who had returned from three years flying bombers over Europe, and they had bought the Golden Nugget Hotel at Timber Creek. Phyllis wasn't too keen about being a publican's wife because, in spite of her upbringing on the run-down farm, she had developed into a bit of a snob. Funny how that happens sometimes. Human nature, I suppose. In fact poor old Ron used to reckon that she was so uppity sometimes that he couldn't even fart in his own house.

After leaving school Phyllis had gone over to Christchurch and done her hairdressing training, which was a bit of a waste, really, as there wasn't much call for a women's hairdresser in Timber Creek. She complained to Ron about this and said that, but for the pub, she could be running a chic little salon in the city. But love does funny things and Ron looked so handsome in his flying officer's uniform.

'He was awarded the DFC, you know,' she would say proudly. Ron wished she wouldn't go on about it so much: he just wanted to forget about the war and get on with running the Golden Nugget.

Meanwhile, Ernie spent the next twenty years in Canterbury working in woolstores, freezing works, and even on a night cart – not that the night cart job lasted very long. After falling over with a full pan on a frosty brick path he decided he'd had enough of that shitty job!

He was always a hail-fellow-well-met type of guy and never had problems getting into conversation with blokes in pubs and on trains, etc. One day, while having a few beers in a pub in Moorhouse Avenue, he met up with a part Maori bloke called Sonny Watere. Sonny had come down from Ruatoria and had picked up a fencing contract over on Banks Peninsula. He needed a mate and, you guessed it, Ernie started another job.

'Piece of cake this one, Ernie, eh,' said Sonny as they arrived at a farm in Sonny's battered old Bedford truck. The farm was situated right at the top of a long steep-sided valley and was reached by a tortuous winding road from the beach where the valley met the sea. The road taxed Sonny's old Bedford to the hilt and Ernie was very relieved when they rolled into the farmyard. At times he thought the old bus was going to give up the ghost and quietly expire by the roadside. Of course, Sonny's driving didn't exactly inspire confidence either: he hardly stopped talking from the time they left Christchurch and spent a lot of his time waving his arms about to prove a point. When Ernie remonstrated about this, Sonny laughed and said, 'She's right, Ernie, the old Beddy just about drives herself.'

They settled into the shearers' quarters, where they were to live during the contract. After unpacking their gear off the truck and making a brew of tea, they rolled smokes and went over to have a look at the heap of posts, strainers, battens and wire which was stacked up beside the shearing shed.

'How are we goin' to get this stuff up there?' asked Ernie pointing up the hill to where Sonny had indicated the fence was to be erected. 'The old Beddy won't go up there.'

'Doesn't have to,' replied Sonny. 'Cocky's goin' to lend us his old T20 crawler and trailer to cart the stuff up the hill.'

'Hope you can drive a crawler, Sonny,' said Ernie ' 'Cos I can't.'

'Yeah, mate, nothin' to it,' replied Sonny 'Drove a D8 for six months on land developments near Rotorua, eh.'

They heard the gate click and saw the cocky, surrounded by thick clouds of smoke from his pipe, approaching from the house.

'G'day,' he said as he emerged from behind the smoke.

' 'Ow yer goin'?' said Sonny. 'This is me mate, Ernie.'

The cocky nodded at Ernie and said, 'Now I want a good job done, see. No short cuts and yer clean up after. I've had the bulldozer in to clear the line so she should be plain sailing.'

'Don't worry, boss,' assured Sonny, 'Me and Ernie will do a good job for yer. As soon as we've finished smoko, we'll take a load up the hill. Does the old T20 run on petrol or power kerosene?'

'Start her up on petrol and switch over on to kero, and mind she's hot enough before yer switch over.'

'Yeah, she'll be right boss,' said Sonny.

They went back over to the hut and drank their tea.

'Okay Ernie,' said Sonny, throwing the dregs from his cup out the door and narrowly missing the cocky's daughter, who happened to be leading her pony past the door. 'Best get crackin', eh.'

Sonny cranked up the reluctant old tractor, hooked on the

trailer, and drove over to the heap of fencing material.

He let the engine fast idle to ensure that it would be hot enough to switch to kerosene. They threw posts, battens and wire, together with Sonny's wire jinny and tools, on to the trailer.

'Okay Ernie, all aboard,' shouted Sonny as he switched off the petrol and turned on the kerosene tap. The tired old engine gave a couple of coughs, blew out a puff of blue smoke and settled down to an uneven idle.

'Bit of a bloody wreck,' said Sonny to himself. 'Hope the track gear is okay. Don't want the old bus to throw a track halfway up the hill.'

He climbed into the seat and adjusted an old chaff sack filled with straw so that it protected his behind from a protruding spring. He selected third gear, opened the throttle, and drove over to a gate in a row of macrocarpa trees through which the track went up the hill. At the gate he stopped and waited. Ernie was busy admiring the scenery and looking anywhere but at the gate.

'C'mon, Ernie!' yelled Sonny. 'Open the ruddy gate, will yer?'

'Aw sorry,' said Ernie as he jumped off the trailer and skidded in a big cow pat, landing heavily on his behind. Sonny laughed and said, 'Have to get you a parachute if yer goin' to do that every time, eh?'

Ernie grabbed a handful of dry grass and wiped most of the cow dung off his old strides; he then opened the gate and Sonny drove through. They arrived at the fence line without further incident and, as Sonny drove along, Ernie threw the material off according to Sonny's instructions. When it was all gone, Sonny headed back down to the yard for another load. By nightfall they had all the material out on the line.

They ate a tea of chops, potatoes and carrots, expertly cooked by Sonny on the old wood range in the hut. Sonny went out to his truck and came back in with a couple of bottles of beer, one of which he passed to Ernie.

'There's yer ration, mate,' he said.

'Aw gee,' complained Ernie, 'I thought we might go to the local pub for a few tonight. Nothin' to do here.'

'No pubs till she's finished, Ernie – got to get an early start in the mornings and put in some long days: it's the only way yer can make these jobs pay. I want to get this one cleaned up quick. I'm goin' up to Kaikoura after this. Subdivision fence on a station to do. Might take yer along if you're up to it.'

That evening they played a few games of cards and retired early to their bunks. Next morning they were up bright and early, woken by the dawn chorus of a couple of magpies over in the macrocarpa trees.

'Noisy blighters, them things,' said Ernie.

'Sure are,' agreed Sonny, 'Not many native birds left down here. You pakeha jokers must have killed them all off.'

After breakfast they cut some sandwiches, filled a couple of flasks with tea for their smokos and lunch, and set off up the track. Sonny set a fast pace and it wasn't long before Ernie started to lag behind.

'Not so fit, eh Ernie?' said Sonny. 'Never mind, mate, by the time we've finished this job I'll have yer runnin' up the hill.'

As they reached the top of the ridge, the heat from the sun was making them sweat profusely and Ernie was starting to wonder if this fencing caper was really his thing. Still, he would have to stick it out for a while; couldn't let Sonny down at this stage. If it got too tough he could always plead the old war wound trick: it had got him out of many hard jobs and, with him being a returned soldier, it invoked a lot of sympathy.

Their first job was to put in a strainer post twelve feet from the boundary fence, to allow for a gateway. The ground was baked hard after the summer drought and even the crowbar made little impression on it.

'By Korri, I hope she's not goin' to be like this all the time,' said Sonny, wiping the sweat from his brow with his arm. 'Won't make any money out of it at this rate. Here we are at smoko and we haven't even got the first strainer in yet.'

Ernie was by this time feeling pretty knackered. All the bad beer of the last few weeks was weeping from every pore and he was wondering if he might have to introduce the old war wound earlier than he had envisaged.

'Real bastard,' said Sonny.

'Yeah, real bastard,' agreed Ernie.

'Yer know, Ernie, it's the worst bastard I've ever worked on – even worse than the one me and me coussie Witi worked on up the East Coast near Tolaga Bay. There, mud was the problem – yer could dig the holes okay but they kept fillin' up with water and yer couldn't get yer posts in firm. We strained up the first strainer and pulled it right out of the ground, even though we'd footed 'er proper an' that. Yeah, real bastard all right.'

By lunch-time Ernie was getting his second wind and reckoned he might last out the day. They had the first strainer footed and rammed in the ground and the stay fitted. Digging the hole for the second strainer was a whole lot better, so things didn't look quite so bad. They ran out a wire, strained it up and then started to put in the intermediate posts. The first three were quite good digging and the men became almost optimistic again; but that was a bit premature as the ground once more became rock hard.

'Bugger this for a joke, Ernie,' said Sonny in disgust. 'Where's me chain-saw? I'll show yer what we do at times like this.'

Small chain-saws were just coming into their own in New Zealand at that time, taking over from the clumsy old two-man jobs, and Sonny's was his pride and joy. He started it up and cut about eighteen inches off the butt end of the post, so that instead of there being thirty inches in the ground, there would only be about twelve inches. By doing this with each post where the digging was hard they made good progress. They threw the offcuts down the hill into a patch of manuka scrub.

'Cripes, Sonny,' said Ernie. 'Won't the cocky go crook about us doin' this?'

'Nar,' replied Sonny. 'Bugger will never know. We'll strain 'er up good and tight and if he ever does find out we'll be long gone.'

By evening knock-off time, they had all the posts in on the first strain and the wires run out, strained up and stapled on.

'See, Ernie,' said Sonny, grabbing a post and trying to rock it – mind you, he made sure it was one that they hadn't cut short – 'She's as solid as me old mum's Christmas puddings. The cocky'll never know.' Just as they were knocking off and gathering up their coats and lunch gear, they heard a horse snort and the cocky rode over the ridge on a chestnut mare, followed by a couple of dogs, one of which lifted its leg on the nearest post.

'G'day,' greeted Sonny brightly. 'Good job eh Boss? Old dog reckons so, any way. Dogs always have a leak on something they reckon is good.'

'Yeah, well this time the dog's wrong. I don't know what you jokers think yer playin' at,' said the cocky in an angry tone of voice, 'but down in the gully there's a whole lot of eighteen inch lengths of silver pine. I reckon you lazy bastards have been cuttin' the bottoms off the posts and throwin' 'em down into the scrub. What yer don't realise is that, being round, a lot of them rolled right through the scrub and landed on the track in the bottom of the gully.' He got off his horse and, grasping one of the intermediate posts, pulled it out of the ground. The next one came out just as easily.

'You mongrels,' he roared. 'Thought yer could put one across me, did yer? Well yer can pack yer gear and get off the place and don't show yer useless faces around here again.'

'Yeah, well the ground was hard, like,' explained Sonny, 'and we didn't want you to think we were slacking on it.'

'Just get the hell off the place. I want yer away from here by tonight.'

'Any chance of getting the old tractor to cart our gear down the hill?' asked Sonny.

'No,' said the cocky. 'Yer can carry it down and I hope yer rupture a gut doing it too. Now get off the bloody place before I really lose me temper.' He got back on his horse, called to his dogs, and rode off down the hill.

So that was the end of Ernie's brief fencing career. Sonny wanted him to go up to Kaikoura but Ernie declined. Somehow he didn't seem to be cut out to be a fencer and he had the feeling that Sonny might not be the most reliable of mates. Sonny took him back to Christchurch, handed him a few quid for his day's efforts, and they went their separate ways.

CHAPTER FOUR

A lot of you older folk will remember the days when tough wiry guys went out into the bush, the hills and the mountains to shoot deer. The deer had reached pest proportions and were merrily chomping their way through the undergrowth in our native forests and were competing with the sheep for the available feed. Something had to be done about it and so the culling of the deer by these shooters was introduced. Our friend Ernie was among these deer cullers for a short time; but more of that later.

As time went by these deer became valuable; the meat was in demand overseas; all sorts of interesting things were made out of the skins; and randy old Oriental gentlemen reckoned that the velvet in the antlers, when ground into a powder, was an aphrodisiac. Well, I ask you! So deer culling ceased and deer farming commenced. Crazy guys in little bubble helicopters scoured the hills and mountains for these deer, netting, tranquillising and bulldogging them, then hooking them on below the chopper and flying them to the nearest deer farm. Sales of six foot netting and tanalised posts boomed and a new industry blossomed in the land.

Back on the dole again and doing whatever jobs he could pick up after his short venture into fencing, Ernie often had to live rough; sleeping most nights in empty railway carriages and vans down near the station. He was having a beer in his favourite watering-hole in Moorhouse Avenue, when down at the end of the bar he saw a discarded newspaper. Ernie picked it up and it happened to be open at the 'Situations Vacant' page; so Ernie, having been idle long enough, glanced down the columns. About halfway down he read: 'Fit men, who are used to hill country conditions and who are good shots, are required for deer culling operations throughout New Zealand. Good wages and all food, ammunition and rifles provided. Apply to the Wildlife Division, Internal Affairs Dept.' There was a phone number.

Ernie, on impulse, which was the way he did most things, went over to the phone on the bar and dialled the number.

'Good morning,' said a honeyed voice, 'Internal Affairs Dept. Wildlife Division, Angela speaking.'

'Yeah. G'day,' said Ernie in his best cultured voice. 'I'm ringin' about the deer cullin' job, like.'

'Hold the line, please, and I'll put you through to Mr Frame,' said the voice.

'Frame speaking. How can I help?' asked a business-like voice.

'Me name's O'Neil,' replied Ernie, 'and I'm ringin' about the deer cullin' job.'

'Yes all right, Mr O'Neil. Perhaps you could come round and see me at, let me see, yes, I'm free at 2 pm. How would that suit you?'

'Yeah, reckon I could make it at two,' replied Ernie. 'I'm a bit tied up this mornin' and I've got an appointment at twelve-thirty but, yeah, two o'clock would suit good. See yer then.' He put down the receiver. The idea of Ernie having an appointment was really quite ludicrous, but he believed that saying he did would impress people. Promptly at two o'clock he walked up the stairs and into the office. He spurned the use of the lift, not trusting 'them things'. He went up to the reception desk. The shapely blonde behind the desk stopped typing and, flashing a toothpaste smile at Ernie, said 'Yes?' Ernie, hearing her speak, realised that she was the owner of the honeyed voice he had heard on the phone that morning. 'Not a bad lookin' sheila,' he thought, 'that's if yer like them painted dolls.'

'Me name's O'Neil and I've come abut the deer cullin' job,' said Ernie. 'I was to see a joker called Frame.'

'Just take a seat, Mr O'Neil,' she said, 'and I'll see if Mr Frame is free.'

She picked up the phone and, pressing a button, said, 'Mr O'Neil is here, Mr Frame.' She listened for a moment, then replaced the receiver and said to Ernie, 'Just go through that door. He'll see you now.'

Ernie walked through the door into a half-acre office, remembering to remove his old hat as he did so. A neatly suited man of about forty-five was just getting up from a large mahogany desk, the size of which was admirably suited to the room. There was a large leather lounge suite, an ornate coffee table and an open cocktail cabinet at the end of the room opposite the desk. Ernie eyed the contents of the cocktail cabinet and hoped that the man might just crack his whip to prospective deer cullers.

'Ah, Mr O'Neil,' said the man in a hearty voice. 'I'm Frame, Director for the South Island. Nice to meet you. Do please sit down. No, not over there – at the desk would be more convenient and appropriate, don't you think?'

Ernie realised that he was not going to be entertained down at the leather end of the room. Before resuming his seat behind his desk Mr Frame went over and closed the cocktail cabinet. Ernie then concluded, quite rightly, that he wasn't going to get a drink either. He slid into a straight-backed chair at the desk.

Mr Frame looked a little surprised to see someone come into his office attired as Ernie was: his clothes were not only old and tattered, they were also pretty filthy. The stain of the cow manure from Banks Peninsula still showed on his jeans: a bit of a wipe with cold water hadn't done much good. Still, Mr Frame had seen some fairly hard men come in for interviews for the deer culling jobs. He pushed a box of cigarettes across the desk but Ernie declined, saying, 'I'll roll me own, thanks. Don't like them things.'

'I don't usually do these interviews,' said Mr Frame. 'Our Mr Stone is normally the man you would see but he is away on leave so I'm helping out. So you want to be a deer culler? Have you done much shooting?'

'Spent nearly six years over in the Middle East and Italy shootin', mate.' said Ernie. 'Not shootin' deer but shootin' at Jerries and Ities.'

'Oh, a returned serviceman, are you? Must look after you boys', said the man in a patronising tone of voice. 'Didn't get away myself. Essential industry, don't you know? Anyway, there's a block over on the West Coast up the Ranginui River that needs cleaning out. Do you know the Coast?'

'Born and bred there,' said Ernie. 'Suits me okay to go over there.'

'That's good then,' said Mr Frame. 'The wages are ten pounds a week and found plus five shillings a tail. No skinning to do now, just collect the tail. You may take what meat you require for yourself. We allow three cartridges per animal; after that, you provide your own. You are responsible for wet weather gear and boots, but if you don't have them, the department will provide them and deduct the cost from your pay. We provide a sleeping-bag and rifle, ex-army .303. Sometimes it may be necessary to live in a tent camp. Have you done much camping out, Mr O'Neil?'

'Listen, mate,' said Ernie, getting a trifle annoyed at the pompous twit, 'if you had been overseas as long as me, you wouldn't ask a silly bloody question like that.'

'No sorry, very stupid of me,' apologised the man. 'Can you leave for the Coast straight away? We want to get this block cleaned up as soon as possible. With the winter approaching and the leaseholder having agreed to muster his cattle off the river flats for a month, the sooner we get on to it the better.'

'Leave tomorrow if yer like,' offered Ernie.

'Oh, jolly good,' said Mr Frame. 'We've got a young chap over there in Port Thompson waiting for a mate so I'll send you in with him. He's apparently had a lot of experience in the high country, mustering, shooting, etc. Sounds like a good type of fellow. I'll book you a seat on tomorrow morning's railcar.' He rang the railway booking office and booked the seat. He took out a form and wrote briefly on it before passing it to Ernie.

'Your travel warrant,' he said. 'You can exchange it for a ticket at the booking office tomorrow morning. Right. That's about the lot then, good luck'.

Ernie realised that the interview was at an end so he got up and went over to the door. Mr Frame once again had his head down and was immersed in the papers on his desk.

'Cripes,' thought Ernie. 'He's forgotten me already. What a poncy job, sittin' behind that big desk all day. Wonder how he would go out in the bush? Bloody useless, I bet. Still I suppose the job has some compensations – coot probably gets first call at the blonde bint in reception.'

Ernie made for the nearest pub to have a couple of beers to celebrate: unusually for him, he stopped at two – but only because he was just about stony-broke. Still, he had a job to go to and that was something. Being in the bush he might be able to cut back on the grog and save some money; always an optimist and full of bright ideas was our Ernie. Next morning he rolled up his few belongings into his old army kitbag and left the Salvation Army lodgings where he had spent the previous two nights. The man in charge was really pleased that Ernie had a job to go to and said that he hoped Ernie would be a bit more abstemious in the future.

'Have to be, Captain,' said Ernie cheerfully. 'Not many pubs in the bush.'

He went off down to the railway station, running late as usual, and just caught the railcar as it was pulling out of the station. The guard yelled him for boarding a moving train.

'Well, if you'd waited for a bloke I wouldn't *have* to get on a movin' train. Anyway, yer trains run that slow it's hard to tell if they're movin' or not,' Ernie yelled back.

When the guard came through the train calling for tickets,

Ernie passed him the travel warrant.

'Hey, what's this?' growled the guard. 'Why didn't yer get this changed for a ticket at the station?'

'Didn't 'ave time,' explained Ernie. 'Yer started yer train too soon. Anyway it's all I've got. Yer can take it or leave it. I'm headin' over to the Coast to clean up them deer over there. Gettin' real bad they are. Eatin' all the bush and that.'

'Should put yer off at Springfield,' said the guard.

'You and how many others?' retorted Ernie.

'Yeah, all right,' said the guard, seeing that the other passengers were starting to laugh at him, 'but you watch it, mate.'

'Yeah, you too, with knobs on,' said Ernie, who was getting thoroughly hacked off with the nit-picking little twit. He settled back in his seat and ignored the guard, who went on through the carriage calling out, 'Tickets please. All tickets please.'

It was a long time since Ernie had been back to the Coast and he thoroughly enjoyed the journey through the mountains into the lush rainforest and green farmlands of his birthplace.

At Ngaio, after coming through the tunnel, he really felt that he was home and celebrated by spending almost all his remaining money on a lukewarm pie and a cup of railway tea at the refreshment room. The rest of the journey went without incident – except when two old ladies complained to the guard about Ernie smoking in a non-smoking compartment.

'I told yer to watch it,' said the guard.

'Sorry, mate. Sorry, ladies,' said Ernie. 'Didn't know it was one of them non-smokers, like. Do yer want me to move into a smoker?'

'No room in there,' said the guard. 'If yer want a smoke, go out on the platform.'

That ended that little episode and Ernie studiously avoided looking at the two little old ladies by enjoying the scenery out of the window.

Soon afterwards, the railcar pulled into Port Thompson.

CHAPTER FIVE

As Ernie left the train, he received a black look from the guard. He shouldered his kitbag, made his way out of the station and paused at the door to look over towards the river. There were two Union Company colliers tied up to the wharf, taking on coal. He heard a steam train and turned to see an old tank loco, hauling a rake of coal wagons, crossing the bridge over the Thompson River. 'Hasn't changed much,' he mused, as he set off up Main Street, which was where he judged the Wildlife office might be. 'Bit more traffic and a few more buildings but, yeah, she hasn't changed much. Anyway, it's better like this with not too many changes. That's the trouble with them big cities; they're always rippin' things down and changin' the place around. Yer don't know whether you're Arthur or Martha.'

He stopped a passer-by and asked, 'Hey, mate, where's the Internal Affairs Office? You know, the Wildlife outfit?'

'About a couple of hundred yards down on the left. Yer can't miss it,' said the man. 'Hey aren't you Ernie O'Neil what used to live at Timber Creek?'

'Yeah, that's me,' said Ernie sounding a bit puzzled.

'Don't yer remember me, Ernie? Ces Draper.'

'Hell, yes!' exclaimed Ernie, 'I ain't seen yer for a long time. Didn't recognise yer. 'Ow yer goin'?'

'Good, Ernie,' said Ces. 'Hey, don't tell me yer goin' deer cullin.' Watch out for that niggly bastard Jamieson what's in charge up there. Put one across yer while yer thinkin' about it, he will. Too miserable to cast a shadow. He's one pest they ought to cull out. Not popular around here, he isn't. Real bloody civil servant. He's cross-eyed too, so just watch out. When yer think he's lookin' at someone else, he's really watchin' you, so don't go tryin' to nick a pair of boots or something when he's not lookin', because he'll have yer.'

'Okay Ces,' said Ernie. 'Thanks for the warnin'. That's the trouble with some of these blighters. Yer can't trust 'em, can yer? Anyway I'd better get goin' and sign in or whatever yer have to do. See yer, Ces.'

'Yeah, Ernie,' replied Ces. 'Keep in touch, mate. I'm still livin' at Timber Creek. Got a wife and a coupla kids and a job in the saw mill. You married, Ernie?'

'Nah,' said Ernie. 'Haven't got much time for women. Necessary evil, I suppose. If they didn't nag so much they'd be okay, I guess, but it's do this and do that all the time. No thanks, mate, I'm stayin' single.' Ernie waved his hand and continued up the street.

Ces thought, 'Fancy seeing old Ernie again. Looks like he's let himself go a bit with his dirty old clothes and that flowing beard. What he probably wants is a good woman to sort him out in spite of what he says about them. Oh well, it takes all sorts, I guess.'

Ernie didn't like Ces's description of Jamieson one little bit; sounded like a real bastard. 'Looks like I might have to sort him out for a start,' he said to himself as he arrived at an old wooden building set back from the street. It had a faded sign over the door which informed anyone interested that it was the office of the Wildlife Division, Internal Affairs Dept. The weatherboards were fighting a losing battle trying to hold on to the flaking barn-red paint which had once covered the building. The roof was rusty corrugated iron and the spouting sagged badly in the middle. The whole place was festooned with cobwebs and moss.

'Cripes,' remarked Ernie to himself as he walked up two worn steps to the door. 'She's a bit different to that city slicker's office over in the smoke. Bet there's no flash lookin' sheila behind the desk here.' Pushing open the solid old kauri door, he went inside.

Across the match-lined room there was a wooden counter, behind which a lean red-headed bloke was stacking boots on a shelf.

'What do you want?' he asked in a surly voice. Ernie could see that he was cross-eyed all right because, even though he was addressing Ernie, he was looking at a point away over Ernie's right shoulder.

'Me name's O'Neil,' said Ernie. 'I've just got 'ere from Christchurch to go deer cullin.'

'Aw yeah, I got a ring on the phone about you,' said the man. 'You're going down to the Ranginui River block. Frame said you might need some boots and wet weather gear. You can't go climbing around the mountains in tennis shoes. She rains like a bastard most of the time up the Ranginui Gorge so you'll be getting plenty wet. Why the hell you blokes want to come over here to work in the wet sure beats me. Your joints will rust up down the Ranginui, mate.'

'Know all about the Coast, mate,' said Ernie. 'I was born and bred here on a farm up at the top of the Thompson River flats, so I know what rain is.'

'Yeah, well, don't say I didn't warn yer,' said the man. 'What size boots do you take? We've got some ex-army ones here.'

'Size five and a half,' replied Ernie, 'and no wisecracks about me small feet – had enough of that in the army.'

'Don't give a toss what size yer feet are. Wouldn't expect a little bloke like you to have big feet anyway. Here. Try these on,' and the man passed over a pair of almost new boots. Ernie tried them on but they were too small.

'Better try the six,' said the man, looking to the left and picking up a pair on the right.

'Tricky bastard in a fight,' thought Ernie. 'You wouldn't know who he was aiming to hit.' Aloud he said, 'They fit good.'

'Now here's yer parka, leggings, sleeping-bag and pack. You can pick 'em all up in the morning. You'll get yer rifle then too. Now just sign here so we can deduct the cost of these items off yer wages. Be here at eight o'clock sharp. Right, O'Neil, I'll see you tomorrow.' The man turned round and, completely ignoring Ernie, went back to stacking boots.

'Where do I stay tonight? And can I have an advance on me pay?' asked Ernie.

The bloke looked round and said, 'I'll give you a fiver tomorrow. You can stay at the Crown Hotel. The Department will pick up the tab for a bed and meals, but no booze. Understand?'

'Yeah,' said Ernie as he walked out the door. It looked like no beer tonight – unless he put across the old digger story. It had worked wonders in the past for a few free beers.

Next morning after a good breakfast, Ernie walked up the street to the office, glancing in shop windows as he went. He arrived at the office to find a Land Rover with a canvas canopy on the back parked outside the door. It had 'wildlife' painted on the door. Jamieson was standing beside the vehicle looking at his watch. Beside him stood a youth of about twenty. He was lean, about six foot two, and looked to be full of confidence.

'Gawd,' thought Ernie. 'It looks like I'm saddled with this useless twit.'

'Where've you been?' roared Jamieson. 'You're fifteen minutes late.' From the direction the cross-eyed Jamieson appeared to be looking, Ernie concluded that he was addressing the youth.

'I'm talking to you, O'Neil,' said Jamieson. 'I said you're late.'

'Sorry, mate. It's yer cross-eyes, yer see,' said Ernie with his usual tact, 'I thought yer was talkin' to the kid, here. Anyway there's no need to get shirty about it. It weren't my fault. The cook slept in, see, and breakfast was late and I wasn't goin' to miss me breakfast for any bloody government department.'

Ernie didn't think it necessary to mention that the reason the cook slept in was the session that they had had last night. Ernie had, very successfully, put across the 'old soldier' story and the cook had paid for Ernie's drinks all evening. Not being such an experienced soak as Ernie, the cook had to be carried off to bed in the wee small hours and was suffering from a monumental hangover in the morning.

'Huh,' grunted Jamieson. 'Anyway, this is your mate, Christopher Channelle.'

'How do you do, Mr O'Neil?' said the youth in a cultured voice as he extended a hand to Ernie.

'G'day,' replied Ernie, taking the proffered hand and squeezing it in a grip of steel which made the youth squirm.

'Oh, I say, do be careful, Mr O'Neil,' said the youth as he massaged his hand.

'Mate,' said Ernie, 'if me and you are goin' to work together, you'll soon learn me name's Ernie. Where did yer get the name of Channel from anyway? Never heard that one before.'

'Not Channel, Ernie, Channelle,' said the youth. 'You see, my paternal great, great grandparents were French. They came out to New Zealand in the early days and settled on a property up the Rakaia Gorge. It's still in the family; now run by my uncle. That's where I gained my mustering and deer stalking experience.'

'Huh, bloody frog, eh?' said Ernie with contempt. 'Met a few of them buggers in the war. Don't have much time for 'em.'

'Oh, come on, Ernie,' said Christopher. 'They were on the same side, don't you know?'

'And what would you know?' sneered Ernie. 'Anyway, they packed it in pretty quick in 1940.'

'C'mon, you jokers,' said Jamieson. 'Stop your arguing and get in the Land Rover. We've got a long way to go and I want to be back home here tonight, not in three weeks' bloody time. Incidentally, here's your five quid, O'Neil. Right. In you get.'

'You sit in the middle, sonny, and then yer won't fall out,' said Ernie.

Jamieson climbed into the driver's seat, fired up the engine and drove out on to the road. He turned to the youth and said, 'Are you okay for money, Chris?'

'Christopher, please, Mr Jamieson,' said the boy. 'Yes, I have sufficient funds for my immediate needs, thank you.'

'By Gawd,' thought Ernie. 'I've got a proper prick here. How the hell me and him are goin' to get along I don't know. I'll have to learn the lanky sod a thing or two.'

Jamieson and Ernie hardly spoke during the two hour drive to the Ranginui River, young Christopher talking enough for all three of them about his ability as a musterer, shooter, stock manager and every other thing you could think of. The only time he shut up for a few moments was when he had been holding forth about playing rugby at the flash boarding-school he had attended in Christchurch and Ernie said, 'Suppose yer were good at that too, were yer?'

'No; as a matter of fact the fundamentals of the game quite eluded me,' replied Christopher. 'Actually, my mother didn't like me playing such a rough game and, besides, I suppose one can't expect to be good at everything.'

'What, even you, sonny boy?' asked Ernie sarcastically.

A few minutes later they reached the Ranginui River Bridge.

'Well, this is where we leave the main road and head inland,' said Jamieson, swinging the Land Rover left on to a shingle road that headed toward the distant mountain ranges. The road wound round the edge of a bluff high above the river and descended down on to a large flat, which extended inland for some considerable distance each side of the river. Well-kept dairy and beef cattle farms, protected by stopbanks, lined both sides of the road as it headed toward the bush-clad foothills. Herds of Friesian and Jersey cows grazed the lush pastures and prime Herefords lay in the shade of giant totara, rimu and kahikatea trees, contentedly chewing their cuds. Two men, working on a fence beside the road, waved as the Land Rover went past. Their dog took off after the vehicle, barking loudly, but soon gave up the uneven race and returned to supervise the fencing job from the shade of a patch of rushes.

After about half an hour on the dusty road, they arrived at a gate. Beyond the gate a rough track disappeared into the bush. On the other side of the road there was a gateway in the road and a drive leading off to a big old house surrounded by giant rhododendrons and camellias.

'Open the gate Ernie,' ordered Jamieson. As he got out, Ernie thought things must be looking up: he was Ernie now to Jamieson. Maybe he was getting fed up with the wonderful Christopher too.

'This track,' continued Jamieson as Ernie got back into the Land Rover after closing the gate, 'goes on for about a couple of miles to the Ranginui Flats Hut, which is where you jokers will be based. It belongs to the Hobsons, who lease the Ranginui Run. Not bad old blokes. Bit eccentric at times, especially Ned. That's their house we passed at the gate back there. The two brothers live there with their sister, Katie. She rules the roost and goes out mustering with the best of them. She's seventy if she's a day and she sits a stock horse like she was born in the saddle, which she probably was. Shoots like a marksman too. Been a widow for a number of years. A real tough cookie is Katie.'

The track started to deteriorate and Jamieson engaged four-wheel drive as the vehicle lurched and bumped its way along the track. Young Chris had quietened down a bit since they had hit the rough stuff.

'Young twit probably thought it was tarseal all the way,' Ernie said to himself.

After a couple of miles of bumping over ruts, rocks and tree roots, the bush disappeared and the gorge through which they had been travelling widened out into extensive river flats still in their native state. Away in the distance the flats ended at the foothills below the ramparts of the Southern Alps, capped in their eternal snow. The Ranginui meandered across the flats in numerous streams. Giant logs and stumps, stranded well above the watermark, bore witness to the raging floods which sometimes came down the river after heavy rain in the alps. Hereford cattle in mobs of a dozen or so contentedly grazed the plentiful native grasses with which the flats were covered. A brace of paradise ducks rose up in front of the vehicle, honked their way across the flats to land on a shingle bank in the river, and turned their gaze upon the intruders, ready to take wing again should it be necessary. A mob of hinds, shepherded by an old stag, lifted their heads and loped away into the shelter of the bush.

'Ned and Willie Hobson are going to muster the cattle off the flats tomorrow morning. They don't want 'em there when you jokers are shooting,' said Jamieson. 'Also, they want to pick out some for the Ranginui sale next week.'

The track turned sharp left and headed in the direction of the tall timber where the flats ended and the bush-clad foothills began. Situated beneath three large totara trees was a hut. The walls were made of rough-sawn unpainted timber and the roof was rusty corrugated iron. There was a door in one end, a window halfway along one side, and at the end opposite the door, a tin chimney. A lean-to, also of rusty iron, served as woodshed. Jamieson pulled up outside and said, 'Okay, you blokes, we're here. This'll be your home for the next few weeks. We'll unload now, then I'll head back up to Port Thompson. I'll be back in about ten days' time with more supplies. If you're not about, I'll leave everything inside the hut.'

The boy, who had been as quiet as a dead mouse since they left the road, looked around and said, 'Oh, I say, Mr Jamieson, I really don't think I could possibly live in such a horrible place for that long.'

'If you can't stand the conditions you shouldn't have joined,' said Jamieson with contempt. 'I thought you were used to living in the back country. Anyway it's too late to back down now. Ernie'll look after you.'

The Land Rover unloaded, Jamieson climbed in and, with a wave of his hand, drove off down the track.

CHAPTER SIX

'Gosh, Ernie, I don't like this at all,' Chris complained. 'It's so terribly lonely.'

'Huh,' growled Ernie, 'and you a high country boy. Yer should know all about livin' a bit rough from yer time in the musterin' gang you were tellin' us about. In the Flyin' Gang? Like hell yer were. I was in the army with one of them jokers and he was a real hard man. You wouldn't 'ave lasted five minutes with them jokers. Anyway, what say you cut some wood and get a fire goin' and we'll have a brew? I'll stack some of this stuff inside.'

'Is there an axe, Ernie?'

'I don't flamin' know , mate – 'ave a look mate, 'ave a look'.

Ernie watched the boy go round to the woodshed. He was really starting to get fed up with his hoity-toity companion. 'Wish Jamieson had taken him back to Port Thompson,' he mused.

'Here's an axe, Ernie' called the lad.

'Yeah, well use the bloody thing, then,' yelled Ernie in frustration.

As he carried the supplies inside the hut and stacked them in cupboards made out of old kerosene cases, he heard the sound of an axe tapping pathetically at a log of wood.

'Gawd, I'd better go and see what the useless cow is doin', I suppose,' grumbled Ernie. 'That's if we're ever goin' to get a cuppa'. Going round to the woodshed, he saw Chris taking gentle little taps at a knotted old totara log with the axe.

'Cripes, mate!' Ernie exclaimed. 'You'll never split a log like that. You've got to get a straight grained one. An old knotty log like that is only good when yer've got a good fire goin'. Here give me the axe and I'll show yer how, like.'

In a few minutes Ernie had a supply of wood split and ready to carry inside.

'Now,' he instructed. 'Gather up some of them dry twigs there for kindlin' and go in and light the fire. Yer can light a fire, I suppose?'

'Oh yes,' said the lad still full of confidence, well outwardly anyway, 'I used to light the…'

'Yeah I know,' interrupted Ernie. 'You used to light the fires in the musterers' huts on the station.'

He was getting really disgusted by this time. How was he going to put up with the useless coot for ten days? Why did he continue to make out he'd had all the experience in the world when it was so obvious that he had never been in a mustering gang or worked in the high country, or the low country for that matter? Surely the department would have checked out on him a bit. Still wet behind the ears, he was.

'Be interestin' to see how he handles a rifle,' thought Ernie, 'probably put the wrong end to his shoulder and blow his useless head off. Long as it's not mine, it might be a good thing.'

The youth gathered some dry twigs and took them inside. He came back out and asked, 'Do we have any paper, Ernie?'

'What do yer want paper for?' asked Ernie.

'To light the fire with,' replied Chris impatiently.

'Yer don't use paper to light a fire with 'ere, mate.' said Ernie 'Dry twigs, fern or dead grass is what yer use. Any newspaper will be used in the old dunny back in the bush there – if we run out of paper, yer use dry grass or maybe some of that stack of paperback books yer brought with yer.'

A look of horror came over Christopher's face and he said, 'Oh gosh, Ernie, do we have to use such antiquated toilet facilities and newspaper? I've never been used to that sort of thing.'

'Well, you'd better get used to it,' said Ernie. 'That and washin' in the creek or in the tin basin outside, 'cos that's all we've got up 'ere. Yer not at the Ritz now boy. That's all bullshit about you havin' worked in the high country, isn't it? You're a real townie, aint yer?'

'Yes, I'm sorry Ernie,' said the lad looking very crestfallen, 'I only said that to get the job and to cover up my inexperience. You see, I wanted to get away from home to prove myself. My mother has always waited on me hand and foot. I was very delicate as a child, not like my elder brother, who was always robust and seemed to excel in everything he took on.'

'Okay lad,' Ernie said, now feeling a bit sorry for the boy. 'But yer should have said before. Now yer goin' to have to learn pretty damn quick 'cos we're not up 'ere for the holiday and I'm buggered if I'm goin' to do all the work. Right, I'll light the fire and you go and get a bucket of water from the creek.'

That was a task that young Chris seemed able to accomplish without any problems. By the time he got back Ernie had a good fire going. He filled a billy from the bucket and hung it from a wire hook over the fire: the water soon came to the boil. Ernie threw in a part-handful of tea-leaves picked up a stick and tapped the side of the billy.

'That's real billy tea, that is,' said Ernie.

'Why did you tap the side of the billy with a stick?' asked Chris.

'Makes the leaves sink to the bottom,' replied Ernie. 'Don't want 'em floatin' round on top, eh?'

'Gee!' exclaimed Chris, holding out his mug for some tea.

'When we've had our brew we'll go up the river a bit to see if we can bowl over a deer. Keep us in meat for a few days. 'Ave yer ever eaten venison, Chris?'

'Only once when Grandma cooked some on the station. Grandpa shot a deer on the turnips one morning when I was quite small. I found it most enjoyable.'

'Yeah, well, we'll stew ours – except for the back steaks which are real beaut fried in the pan. Reckon you'll enjoy the stew too, especially with some of them carrots and onions in it. I see

Jamieson was quite generous with the spuds, carrots and onions. Do yer want a slice of bread and butter with yer tea?'

'Yes please, Ernie. I'm quite famished,' said the lad.

Ernie cut two generous slices of bread for each of them and slapped on a thick spread of butter.

'There's a tin of plum jam there if yer want some,' said Ernie.

Chris picked up the tin, looked at it and put it down again.

'What's the matter, boy, don't yer like plum jam?' asked Ernie.

'Yes,' replied Chris, looking somewhat embarrassed. 'But I've never had to open a tin before.'

'Stone the crows!' exclaimed Ernie. 'You've got a hell of a lot to learn, ain't yer? Here. Give me the tin and I'll show yer how'

He picked up the tin opener, hardly believing that a joker could be so ignorant, that he couldn't even open a tin of jam. More ignorant than a Romney ewe.

'There yer are, matey,' he said, passing the tin over, 'ave yer really never opened a tin in yer life?'

'No. My mother would never let us have any tinned food,' answered Chris. 'She said it wasn't good for you.'

'Aw, go on,' scoffed Ernie. 'I've lived on tinned food most of me life. Hasn't done me no harm. And meat too, mate. Don't forget the meat. All this talk about health foods is a lot of bull.'

'Yes, well, Ernie,' said Chris. 'That may be so, but you must admit you didn't grow very tall with your type of diet.'

'Okay, kid,' laughed Ernie. 'Point taken. Right, finish yer tea and we'll go up the river and give some deer a fright. 'Ave yer ever had much to do with a .303? And I want the truth this time. Yer don't muck about with guns, boy.'

'No,' confessed Chris. 'In the cadets at college we learnt how to drill and care for a rifle but we never actually fired them. Well, I once fired a .22 on the range in the gym. I didn't really like guns, you see, and mother wouldn't allow them in the house. She said they provoked violence and killed people.'

'Guns don't kill people,' said Ernie. 'People kill people. Anyway yer goin' to 'ave to learn matey, and learn fast. I'll give yer a few lessons tomorrow. Meanwhile you'd better leave yer rifle behind. Walk behind me at all times, keep quiet and do as yer told. Right?'

'Yes,' replied Chris, at long last realising how green he was. He was lucky really, he reckoned, to have teamed up with Ernie who, in spite of his uncouth ways, was quite good-hearted and had the experience to make a good teacher. Christopher was determined that from then on he was going to listen and learn from Ernie. With Ernie in the lead, the two men set off up the track which followed the edge of the bush. Before they had gone far Ernie stopped and said, 'When I signal you to stop, you stop and shut up mighty quick or I'm goin' to be bloody angry. Watch where yer put yer feet 'cos the track looks pretty rough and we don't want yer stumblin' over a big log or somethin' and scarin' the hell out of everythin' around.'

The afternoon was lovely and sunny with hardly a breath of wind. The bush had that sleepy, drowsy look to it as it soaked up the sun. A bellbird sounded a happy note in the adjacent trees as it too showed its delight in such a beautiful day.

'Gosh this is beautiful, Ernie,' exclaimed Chris, 'I didn't know that…'

'Shut up,' said Ernie in a low voice. 'What did I tell yer?'

About half a mile from the hut Ernie stopped and raised his hand. Chris, who had been admiring the scenery instead of looking where he was going, cannoned into Ernie and said in a loud voice, 'Sorry, Ernie, it appears I was not looking where I was going.'

'Shut up, yer useless twit,' said Ernie angrily as two hinds, which had been grazing quietly about two hundred yards away, looked up and dashed away for the safety of the bush. 'Now look what yer've done. You've scared them off. You're more clumsy than a three-legged bull. The wind was right too and we could have stalked them and I could 'ave dropped one, probably two. What you've got to learn, boy, is: when yer deer stalkin', you watch where yer goin' and yer keep yer mouth shut. If yer must speak, yer speak in a whisper and then only if it's important. If it's not, yer shut yer trap. Now for gawd's sake, keep quiet.'

Ernie set off again with a very subdued Chris following behind, keeping his eyes on the track and Ernie's back. He always seemed to do the wrong thing and he did want to please Ernie now that he had admitted that he was such a greenhorn. Of course, if he hadn't told all those lies about his country experience he would never have got the job in the first place, so he had been lucky – now it was just a case of being careful and doing as he was told.

There was plenty of evidence of deer around the numerous deer tracks which led off into the bush. Chris presumed that the deer lived mainly in the bush during the day and came out to feed on the lush native grasses in the late afternoon and evening. As the sun was sinking and the shadows were lengthening they would probably see more deer from now on. When they had covered a further half-mile Ernie raised his hand. Fortunately Chris was watching this time. Ernie pointed to a fine young hind that was standing just clear of the trees listening to a stag roaring in the bush above her. Ernie raised his rifle, took careful aim and fired. The hind reared up, ran a few paces and fell. It kicked feebly for a few moments and then lay still.

'Gee,' yelled Chris. 'You got her, Ernie!'

'Now what did I tell yer about bein' quiet, eh?' asked Ernie. 'Just because I shot a deer yer don't 'ave to tell the rest of New Zealand about it. C'mon, we'll get the tail and a bit of meat and head back to camp.'

'Stew tonight, Ernie?' asked Chris

'Hell, no,' replied Ernie. 'We'll cut the back steaks out and cook 'em up in the pan tonight. You'll find them pretty good kai, lad. The hind legs we'll hang up in a tree for a few days. The old venison's better when she's been hung for a while. Makes it more gamey, like.'

By this time, they had reached the dead hind and Ernie took

out his sheath knife and expertly removed the back steaks, the hind legs and the tail, watched closely by Chris.

'She's in good nick,' remarked Ernie. 'Should be good eatin'. Here yer are, Chris, yer can carry a leg.'

Chris eyed the bloody leg with some trepidation, much to Ernie's amusement.

'Cripes it won't bite yer, mate. Carry it on yer shoulder, like this. A bit of blood won't hurt yer.'

'Aren't you going to skin the animal?' asked Chris.

'Nah,' answered Ernie as he set off for the camp, 'the skins aren't worth bugger-all these days. We've got to leave the carcasses where we shoot them and just take the tail as proof. They used to skin 'em but it took a lot of time and cost more than they were worth. I reckon, though, one of these days they'll be valuable again.' How right he proved to be.

Arriving at the hut, he quickly removed the skin from both legs, closely watched by Chris.

'You can do that next time,' said Ernie. 'Now get me one of them chaff sacks that the supplies came in and we'll hang them up in a tree. That one over there beside the hut will do. The sack will keep the flies away – and the wasps, which seem to be gettin' worse all the time. Never used to see them things but I guess they're here to stay now. As if we didn't 'ave enough pests in this country, what with politicians, civil servants and the like without them things as well. Never mind, lad, when we've shot the last deer, we'll be able to go out and shoot the wasps. Right, that's got that hung up safe and sound. Now you can 'ave a go at cuttin' some more wood. I'm not goin' to do all the work. Don't forget: straight-grained pieces for splittin'. I'll get the fire lit and 'ave a crack at cookin' them steaks.'

Chris disappeared round the back of the hut and shortly afterwards Ernie heard the axe being applied with much more vigour than previously.

'I'll just leave the young blighter alone for a while and see 'ow he goes,' said Ernie to himself. 'Certainly sounds a bit more like it anyway.'

After a while the chopping ceased and young Chris came round the corner with an armful of split wood.

'I say, Ernie,' he said. 'How does that look?'

'Yeah that looks more like it,' said Ernie. 'Bring that lot in and then cut some more. The practise will do yer good.'

Ernie stoked up the fire until he had a good blaze. He took some potatoes out of a bag and with his sharp pocket knife started to peel them into a billy. He added some salt and water and set the billy over the fire. He got out a battered old frying pan, added some fat to it and balanced it on a couple of iron standards, which were placed across the fireplace. When the fat melted he placed the two back steaks in the pan and, rolling a cigarette, settled down to watch the steaks as they sizzled in the pan. He turned them frequently to make sure the cooking was even. He got out two plates and knives and forks and set them on the table. As it was becoming dark he lit a pressure lamp. When the steaks and potatoes were cooked he went to the door and called Chris in from his wood chopping.

'Do believe the young bugger is enjoyin' it,' he chuckled. He called out, 'Come and get it, mate.'

He could see that the sun had sunk down over the Tasman Sea leaving a brilliant glow in the western sky: the sign of another fine day tomorrow. He went back into the hut and dished up the meal, dropping one steak on the dirty floor. Without hesitating he picked it up, brushed the worst of the dirt off it and placed it on Chris's plate.

'He won't notice it in this light,' said Ernie. 'Besides, he probably didn't get his ration of dirt when he was a kid. I bet his old woman wouldn't let her little darlin' get dirty. They reckon everyone has to have his fair share of dirt. I reckon I got my share anyway.'

Chris arrived in with another load of wood which he dropped in the corner beside the fire.

'I've got some more out there' he said proudly .'You know, Ernie, I quite enjoyed doing that. My, that steak certainly smells good.'

''Ave yer tea first, lad, and bring in the rest of the wood later,' said Ernie. 'Meantime get yer chompin' gear round that feed. Soon it will be your turn to cook some tucker. I'll 'ave to learn yer I suppose.'

'I'm afraid so,' said Chris, whose prowess in the culinary department was, like most things, non-existent.

'The Hobsons are goin' to muster the flats tomorrow mornin' so, we won't be able to go shootin' early. The best times are early mornin' and late afternoon. Tell yer what I'll do, boy, is give yer a few lessons on 'ow to handle a rifle. When that joker Jamieson wasn't lookin' I managed to grab a couple of packets of .303 ammo out of a box on the back of his ute, so we've got a few rounds up our sleeves. Now, when we shot that hind I saw a deep gully goin' back into the hills. The bottom looked pretty clear and I reckon we could set up a bit of a range there and let yer fire a few shots. The sound of the shots won't carry too far and scare the hell out of the deer in the valley'. 'Ow's yer tucker?'

'Oh, it's beautiful,' said Chris. 'I think I could finish off with a bit of bread, though.'

''Elp yerself,' said Ernie. 'We'll 'ave to be makin' a bit of camp-oven bread before long. She's good stuff if she's made right.'

It had been a long day so the men retired early: Chris getting into an expensive pair of silk pyjamas, Ernie sleeping in his singlet and underpants. Chris folded his clothes neatly while Ernie flung his in a heap on the floor.

'Yer don't smoke then?' questioned Ernie.

'No,' replied Chris. 'My mother advised against it. She said it was a filthy habit and wouldn't allow any smoking in the house. My father enjoyed his pipe, but he always had to go outside to smoke it.'

'Yeah, that's the trouble with women,' said Ernie. 'On yer back all the time. Well, whether it's a filthy habit or not, I likes me smoke and I ain't goin' outside to have one neither. I always 'ave a few draws before I go to sleep.' And with that he rolled himself a smoke, lit it with a twig from the fire and settled back in his sleeping-bag. Chris climbed into his sleeping-bag and was soon fast asleep.

'I wonder 'ow the young bugger will turn out,' thought Ernie as he lay there turning over the day's events in his mind. 'Snobby bastard; but I guess he means well. Good thing him gettin' away from his mum's apron-strings. Must be a real old dragon, not lettin' the old man smoke in the house. Wonder the old guy didn't push off. If I had a missus like that, which God forbid, yer wouldn't see me for dust. Aw well, as the sayin' goes, it takes all sorts to make the world.' He pinched out his cigarette, turned out the lamp and was soon snoring lustily.

Chris awoke next morning to the smell of wood smoke. Turning over, he saw Ernie squatting down in front of the fire feeding it with sticks and small pieces of wood. A couple of puffs of smoke billowed out into the room. Ernie looked around and said, 'Ah, awake are yer? Thought yer was goin' to sleep all day. Bloody fire's smokin' a bit but once she gets goin' she should be jake. Probably the way the wind is blowin'. Did yer hear that old opossum on the roof last night? Real rowdy bastard he was, felt like firin' a shot at him. If I'd had a .22, I would 'ave but the old .303 might 'ave made a mess of the roof, like.'

'No, Ernie' confessed Chris, as he climbed out of his sleeping bag. 'I didn't hear a thing last night. I slept very soundly. Is there any hot water for a wash?'

''Struth, mate!' exclaimed Ernie. 'What do yer think I am, a bloody valet or somethin'? If yer want hot water, go down to the creek, fill the billy and boil it up yerself. Anyway, what do yer want hot water for? Can't yer just wash in cold?'

'My mother said I should always wash in hot water to cleanse the skin properly,' replied Chris. 'I really don't quite know how

I'm going to manage without my morning shower.'

'Why don't yer go down to the creek and 'ave a swim, then?' scoffed Ernie.

'What a brilliant idea,' said Chris brightly, as he gathered up his towel and toilet bag. 'I haven't got my swimsuit but that probably won't matter up here.'

Ernie cast his eyes to the ceiling and said 'whew' to himself. Out loud, he said, 'Ain't nobody goin' to see yer here, mate.'

Christopher made his way down the track to the creek. Just after it left the bush and trickled across the grassy flat, and before it joined a branch of the river, the stream had been jammed by a big rimu log, creating a small pool. Chris was reminded of the poem 'The Brook' which he had learnt at school.

At this hour of the morning the side of the valley where the hut was situated was still in deep shadow. On the far side the rising sun was spreading itself across the bush-clad slopes of the lower mountains. Further away at the head of the valley, majestic mountains, blanketed in eternal snow, reared up towards the clear blue sky. These extensive snowfields were being painted, as though by a giant brush, in pink and gold as the sun rose higher in the sky. Jagged peaks, so steep that they were almost bare of snow, thrust their way upward to frown down on the world below.

'How beautiful,' said Chris to himself as he gazed at the unfolding scene in awe. 'One never sees perfection such as this in the city. I think I am going to enjoy this life. I will have to listen carefully and learn from Ernie, though. He obviously doesn't suffer fools gladly – not that he would know what that meant. It's a pity I made out I knew so much when in fact I am so ignorant of the things which are important out here. It just shows that a good education and university doesn't mean a lot when you start mixing it with nature. He's a rough old character but I'm sure there's a kindly streak in him, if only I can break through to it. Ah, this pool looks just the ticket for my ablutions.'

He removed his pyjamas and felt the keen morning breeze on his naked body. Throwing his towel over a dead branch which protruded from the log, he entered the water. Knee-deep, he started to soap his body. The chill of the mountain water almost stung his legs and a long shiver went through him.

Suddenly there was a crashing in the bush and out into the open charged three longhorn Hereford steers, followed by a figure on a chestnut gelding. The figure was dressed in a flannelette shirt, jeans, elastic-sided boots and wore a man's old felt hat. Two grey pigtails flew out from under the hat. The woman, for that's what the rider proved to be, drew rein, pulling the horse back on its haunches.

'Wowee!' she exclaimed. 'What have we here?'

Chris, by this time, was trying to cover himself with his hands and had gone red with embarrassment.

'Well,' said the woman. 'It's just as well old Katie Norton's seventy and not seventeen or she'd be down in that pool faster than a bull goes into a paddock of heifers.' She sat on her horse for a moment then continued, 'Aw well, if you're not going to display the interesting bits, a gal might as well push off,' and, digging her heels into the gelding, she galloped after the steers.

Christopher, still feeling embarrassed, stood as though rooted to the spot. He watched old Katie gallop across the flats, rapidly catching up with the steers. Just as they were about to go bush again, she expertly cut off their line of retreat and turned them towards the main mob which, under the guidance of her two brothers, was approaching the track through the bush.

At that, Chris came out of his trance hurriedly left the water, picked up his towel and pyjamas and made for the hut. Ernie, who had seen the whole episode, was still laughing fit to bust.

'Stone the crows, mate,' he said. 'That's the funniest thing I've seen since the handbrake failed on Wally Stone's old Dodge. It was when I was goin' to Timber Creek School. She went careerin' down the sawmill cuttin' with old Wally runnin' behind yellin': 'Whoa, whoa', like it was a horse. Couple o' blokes at the mill, bein' helpful, like, rushed out and threw a piece of six-by-four under the front wheels, thinkin' that might stop 'er. Stopped 'er all right, – trouble was, they only threw it under one front wheel. The old bus slewed round and turned arse over turkey, neat as yer like. Still, we got 'er back on all four wheels again and away she went as good as gold. The one that got the biggest fright was Wally's old spaniel: he was in the cab, see. Wouldn't go near the old Dodge for a couple o' weeks after that. Ah well, better get on, I suppose. Do yer want bacon and eggs for yer breakfast?'

'That sounds just fine, Ernie,' replied Chris, who was now dressed and somewhat recovered from his experience. 'The mountain air certainly does things for one's appetite.'

'Yeah,' said Ernie, who was at a bit of a lost with all this poncy talk. 'You'd better keep yer strength up in case old Katie comes back to see yer again. Wouldn't want to disappoint her now, would yer?'

'Oh dear,' said Chris, a worried look appearing on his face. 'She wouldn't do that, would she?'

'No, she'll be right, mate,' laughed Ernie. 'I reckon old Katie's a bit past it now. Although yer never know. When I was up in Nelson before the war I heard of an old sheila what used to still chase the men at eighty-three – not that she got many takers, like.'

Ernie dished up plates of bacon and eggs and put them on the table. Taking a loaf of bread from the tin, he cut thick slices and said, 'If yer want toast yer can make it yerself over the fire and yer can do the washin' up too, seein' as how I cooked the breakfast while you was givin' the girls a thrill down at the creek. Anyway, eat up and then we'll see 'ow yer go with the .303.'

CHAPTER SEVEN

After breakfast, Chris washed the dishes and then they picked up their rifles and left the hut. Ernie gathered up some empty tins from the heap behind the hut and put them in his pack.

'We'll see if yer can knock a few of them over with yer gun,' he said. Taking the same track as the previous day, they headed up the valley until Ernie stopped and said ''Ere's the side-valley I was tellin' yer about,' and he turned off the main track and entered the valley, Chris following close behind. A small stream, fed by a waterfall at the head of the valley, meandered its way down to the river. The valley floor, like the main river valley, was clear of most vegetation except for grass and fern. A big boulder, shaped like a haystack, lay near where the waterfall tumbled over a rocky escarpment .

'This will do for the butts,' said Ernie. He took the empty tins out of his pack and placed them in a line along the rock. 'We'll sight yer rifle in at 200 yards, but normally the range will be less than that when yer in the bush. You've got to be a good shot to hit anything much over 300, so 200 makes a good average.'

Ernie stepped out 200 paces from the rock and, taking Chris's .303, he set the sights at 200. Taking careful aim at the tin on the left he squeezed the trigger. The bullet ricocheted off the rock about a couple of inches below the tin.

'Firin' a bit low', said Ernie. He adjusted the sights slightly and, working the bolt of the rifle, he aimed and fired again. This time the tin disappeared over the back of the rock.

'That's more like it, boy,' he said, 'Now I'll show yer what to do.' He demonstrated how to fill the magazine and explained to Chris that you never carried the rifle with a round up the spout unless you were about to fire at something; that you always kept the safety-catch on until the last moment; and, most importantly, that you never fired at anything unless you were sure it was a deer.

'Don't want yer to go shootin' yer mate by mistake, do you? Now I'll show yer how to hold yer rifle. Like this, see, tight into yer shoulder or the recoil is goin' to make yer shoulder sorer than a front row forward's after a rough Saturday game. Right, now you'll find that, unless you've gotta make a snap shot, yer better to be lyin' down, kneelin' or restin' the rifle on somethin' like a branch. It's pretty hard to fire accurately for a beginner, shakin' like a virgin on her honeymoon. Right, lie down there and take the rifle like I showed yer and don't forget what I said about holdin' it tight into yer shoulder. And squeeze the trigger, don't pull it. You'll find its got two pressures. Take up the first one and then 'old yer breath while yer squeeze off the shot. As soon as you've fired, work yer bolt to put another round in the chamber as quick as yer can 'cos yer might get another shot. Okay, 'ave a few practice goes, eh, and then we'll give yer a go at the real thing.'

Under Ernie's tuition Chris went through all the motions of firing the rifle.

'I say, this ground is a bit damp to lie on, Ernie,' he complained.

'Yeah, well it would be, wouldn't it? This is the West Coast, mate' said Ernie. 'If yer goin' to work over 'ere you'll often be on wet ground. If it wasn't for the damp, it wouldn't be so green – it would be barren and dry like over the hill: gives a man a thirst to think about it. All right, let's see yer load up and fire yer gun. Just remember everythin' I told yer.'

Chris loaded his rifle under the critical eye of his tutor. He knew that he was being judged by a companion who would be very scathing if he made any mistakes. He was fortunate in that he usually picked things up fairly quickly. Lying down and holding the rifle firmly into his shoulder as Ernie had shown him, he took careful aim at the next tin on the rock. Two hundred yards seemed a long way and the tin looked pretty small through the sights of the rifle. He took the first pressure on the trigger and then, holding his breath for a few seconds, squeezed the trigger. Instead of a loud bang all he heard was a click.'

'Yer mug, yer didn't put one up the spout,' said Ernie in a scathing tone. 'If that had been a stag he would 'ave been in Auckland by now. 'Ave another go and do it right this time.'

Chris worked the bolt of the rifle, feeding a cartridge into the chamber. He cursed himself for being such a fool in front of Ernie. Once more, taking careful aim and remembering the first and second pressure on the trigger, he fired. There was a loud bang and the tin rocked slightly with the wind from the bullet's passing. It must have just missed.

'That's pretty close, Chris,' said Ernie, a new respect creeping into his voice. 'Not bad for a first go. Just aim a fraction to the right and don't forget she's firin' a bit low.'

Chris ejected the spent cartridge and replaced it with a live round. Taking aim once more, he fired and the tin flew up into the air and disappeared behind the rock.

'Hey, that's good, young feller,' said Ernie, pleased that his pupil had done so well. 'Take yer time and 'ave a go at the rest of them tins.'

Chris fired off the rest of the magazine, scoring hits or near misses each time.

'Right, lad,' said Ernie. 'We'll pack it in now. You'll do – bloody natural, you are. Late this afternoon we'll go up the river and see what we can get. You can take the lead and see if yer can get yer first deer. Remember what I said though, no yellin' and watch where yer put yer big feet.'

They returned to the hut, Chris full of joy that he had shot so well. He could already feel a change in Ernie's attitude towards him. He would have to keep on listening to what he was told and remember not to boast about imagined past achievements.

They spent the rest of the day sorting out the camp, cutting firewood and resting. Ernie showed Chris how to clean his rifle and how to care for it. 'Remember it's yer best friend on this job – apart from me, that is,' he joked.

At about three o'clock Ernie said, 'Okay mate. We'll 'ave a brew, then we'll go huntin'.'

'I'll put the billy on,' said Chris who was itching to get up the river after the deer. He waited until the water boiled and then put in a part-handful of tea and tapped it with a stick just as he had seen Ernie do. Ernie looked on with interest and thought to himself, 'Maybe this young bugger isn't goin' to be so bad after all. He learns fast, I'll say that for him.'

Chris poured two mugs of tea and passed one to Ernie saying, 'There you are, mate.'

'Thanks,' said Ernie. He took a sip of the hot tea. 'She's a good brew, boy. Better put me ration of sugar in, though,' and he laced his tea with his usual three teaspoonful.

'Yeah, she is a good brew. We'll make a high country boy of yer yet.'

Chris fairly glowed with pride – praise from Ernie was praise indeed. Things seemed entirely different in their relationship since he had performed so well with his rifle. As he drank his tea he pondered on this and thought, 'I only hope I can shoot as accurately when we go up the river. Must remember everything he told me. I must not get excited. Just stay cool, calm and collected.'

Ernie finished his tea and threw the dregs at the fireplace. The fact that he missed his target by a mile and splattered the dregs all over the chaff sack in front of the fireplace didn't seem to worry him one iota. He laced up his boots, put on his old hat, picked up his rifle and said 'Okay, young feller, grab yer gun and we'll go and shoot some deer.'

Followed by Chris, he set a fast pace up the track along the edge of the bush. There was only a very light breeze blowing and the sun shone down from a cloudless sky. It was quite warm and it was not long before the men were removing their jerseys. After crossing the creek where Chris had had his encounter with old Katie, Ernie said, 'Right, you take the lead, lad, and don't forget what I told yer.'

Chris passed Ernie and they continued on up the track, Chris determined to do everything right. He felt that his whole career as a deer culler depended on what he did over the next hour or so. 'Must keep quiet,' he said to himself. 'Must look where I am going. Must remember what Ernie told me about the rifle.' He kept looking for sign of deer. There were plenty of fresh tracks to be seen.

It was Ernie who saw the deer first. He touched Chris on the shoulder and whispered, 'Out to yer right, mate. Just beside those three big kahikateas over there. Three hinds: and they haven't seen us yet. The wind is right so if we just take it nice and slow, like, we should be able to get a bit closer. You take the first shot. I'll tell yer when.'

With Chris in the lead, they crept slowly along the track until they came to a clump of small trees.

'Stop 'ere,' ordered Ernie quietly. 'I don't reckon we'll get much closer. Set yer sights for three hundred and don't forget she fires a bit low. You take the one on the left and I'll take one of the others. Okay, when yer ready."

Chris knelt down behind one of the small trees and, using a low branch as an aiming rest, he worked the bolt, putting a round in the chamber. Making sure the safety catch was off, he took careful aim and fired. The hind stumbled forward a couple of paces and fell to lie still. Ernie's rifle fired and another deer fell to lie kicking in the grass. The third deer escaped by running away and putting the three kahikateas between her and the hunters.

'There yer are, lad,' said Ernie clapping Chris on the back, 'you've got yer first deer. That was a good shot. C'mon. We'll get the tails and go a bit further up river but I don't reckon we'll see any more for a while. The shots will 'ave scared the blighters off. Do yer feel like steak again tonight?'

'Yes, that would be great.' said Chris who could not believe that he had shot his first deer. I must not get complacent though, he thought. 'Can I have a go at cutting out the steaks?' he asked.

'Sure' said Ernie. He took his knife out of its sheath and passed it to Chris 'We'll 'ave to get yer fixed up with a skinnin' knife too. A stainless steel kitchen knife sharpened up makes a good one. Saw one back at the hut. I'll 'ave a crack at it for yer tonight, if yer like.' Under Ernie's expert guidance, Chris removed the back steaks and put them in his bag.

They went another mile up river but didn't see any more deer within rifle range. There was a mob feeding away across the river but it was flowing too fast for them to cross in safety. If the fine weather continued for a while they might be able to cross over and have a crack at them one day. In the meantime there was plenty of territory to cover on this side of the river.

'Right, let's get home, mate,' said Ernie. 'I'm gettin' ready for me tea.'

They turned and hurried off down the track as the sun was setting over the Tasman Sea: darkness would soon be falling. The sunset coated the whole western sky in brilliant red and orange, promising a fine day on the morrow. When they came in sight of the hut they could see a man on horseback approaching through the dusk. As he caught sight of them, he tugged on the reins and came along the track to meet them.

'G'day,' said the man as he got off his horse. 'Me name's Willie Hobson. Just came over to see if yer okay.'

'That's good of yer,' said Ernie thrusting out his hand. 'I'm Ernie O'Neil and this is me mate, Chris. Can't remember his surname. Some bloody foreign one. Anyway he's a good bloke, and he's just shot his first deer. Dropped 'er at three hundred, he did.'

'Would yous jokers like a beer?' asked Willie. 'I've got a couple of bottles in me saddle-bag.'

'Yeah that'd be good.' replied Ernie. 'I've gotta thirst like a Wellington wharfie on pay night. I reckon me mate, 'ere wants to celebrate, too. Don't yer, lad?'

'That would be wonderful, Mr Hobson, thank you very much. I don't usually drink alcoholic liquors but perhaps this once I may have a small glass,' said Chris.

'Cripes, I'm Willie, lad. None of this mister stuff around 'ere,' said Willie, obviously a bit taken back at the lad's correct speech.

'Don't worry about me mate 'ere and his posh speech; he's a good joker. Might get him to learn me to speak better meself,' said Ernie. Chris reckoned that, if he started to do that, they wouldn't have time to shoot any deer – the way Ernie spoke, you'd have to start from scratch. Perhaps he should modify his way of talking a bit so that he didn't stand out so much from the locals; but then *speech* didn't make a man – just look how much Ernie knew about bushcraft compared to him. What Chris knew wouldn't get him very far if he got lost in the bush.

'Right, let's go up to the hut, then, and we'll sample this brew,' said Willie. When they reached the hut, Willie tied his horse's reins to a sapling growing by the door and, taking a couple of bottles of beer out of his saddle-bag, followed Ernie and Chris inside. Ernie lit the lamp while Chris grabbed three mugs off the shelf and set them on the table.

'I don't see a bottle opener anywhere' he said.

'Cripes, yer don't need a bottle opener to open a bottle of beer. Them things are made to get lost,' said Willie. He held a bottle against the edge of the table and, with a smart blow from his rough old hand, knocked the top off. He poured beer into the mugs and, raising one to his lips, said, 'Good luck', and swallowed it down in about three gulps: obviously an experienced beer drinker.

Ernie said, 'Yeah, all the best', and his beer disappeared in double quick time. Chris, who was not used to drinking, was somewhat slower. 'Drink up, boy,' said Willie. 'Then we can 'ave another one.' Picking up the other bottle, he knocked the top off it and refilled the mugs.

''Ere's to yer first deer, lad,' he said.

'Yeah that goes for me, too,' agreed Ernie.

As he sipped his beer Chris studied old Willie. What he saw was a tall, lean man, straight as a rake handle in spite of his age, which must have been closer to eighty than seventy. What could be seen of his hair under his old felt hat was silver grey. Sharp grey eyes squinted out from below shaggy grey eyebrows. His hooked nose protruded prominently from his face, which was as rugged as the side of Mt Cook. A straggly moustache adorned his upper lip and, from the growth of whiskers on his face, it appeared that he had not shaved for two or three days. His clothes, while being well-worn, were clean and neatly patched; obviously the work of his sister Katie.

Seeing Chris looking at him, he asked, 'Where do yer hail from, boy?'

'Christchurch,' replied Chris.

'Huh,' said Willie. 'Only been there once on me way to camp in 1916. Didn't like the place much – too many people. Been goin' to go back for years to the show and races but never got round to it. Guess the local show and races'll do me now. Old Ned, me brother, he ain't never been to Christchurch. Katie, she's travelled a bit. Been to Dunedin and Wellington, she 'as. Told 'er, I did, that I couldn't see why she wanted to go gallivantin' round so much.' He finished his beer, wiped his mouth with the back of his hand and continued, 'Right, youse jokers, I'm on me way. Katie'll have tea ready and she doesn't like to be kept waitin'. They tell me yer met 'er this mornin', Chris.'

Chris blushed and said, 'I'm sorry, Willie, but I didn't know she would be there.'

'Aw, yer don't want to worry about Katie. Likes to act tough, she does, but she's not a bad old sheila for a sister. Anyway, she's been married so I reckon she's seen it all before. Probably made her day, eh?'

'While yer 'ere, Willie,' said Ernie. 'That bloke Jamieson said you would show us how to get up to the tops from 'ere. He reckoned there was a track up the ridge, like.'

'Aw yeah. Well, she's a bit dark now to show yer much,' explained Willie. 'I'd better come back tomorrow and show yer. Yer see, findin' where the track starts is a bit tricky; 'ow would the mornin' suit yer?'

'Okay Willie, that will do us, won't it Chris?' said Ernie. 'We want to get up there fairly soon while the weather's good. We can shoot the flats when she's wet, like. Jamieson left us a tent fly so we can make a fly camp up there. Then we can 'ave a crack at the bastards first thing in the mornin' and in the evenin'.'

'All right then, but I warn yer she'll be bloody cold up there at night,' said Willie. 'Aw well, I'll see yer tomorrer then. Hooray.' Old Willie went out the door and rode off into the darkness.

'Not a bad old joker,' said Ernie. 'Right, young Chris. We'd better get some tea on. Them worms are startin' to bite. Cripes that beer was good. Hope Jamieson brings some out to us next time. Didn't come up 'ere to sign the pledge. Do yer want to 'ave a go at cookin' the steaks tonight?'

'Probably best if you do them again, Ernie,' replied Chris. 'I'll watch. Last night while you were cooking I was cutting wood.'

'So yer were' said Ernie. 'Right, you watch me then, and I'll learn yer how to do it. I'll 'ave to make bread tomorrer too.'

CHAPTER EIGHT

Next morning as the sun was hitting the peaks opposite, Chris once again made his way down to the creek for his morning wash. A little more cautious this time, he left his underpants on while he bathed. 'They need washing anyway', he said to himself. 'Old Ernie doesn't seem to worry too much about washing. It's a terrific beard that he has got – saves a lot of time and trouble out here in the bush. I think I should consider growing one myself. I don't know what Mother would say, but what the eye doesn't see the heart doesn't grieve about, I suppose. Oh well, I'll try it for a few days. I can always shave it off if it gets too uncomfortable.'

He gathered up his towel and dried himself rapidly, as it was quite cold. Wrapping the towel round himself and picking up the full container of water that Ernie had asked him to fetch, he returned to the hut. When he arrived Ernie was breaking eggs into the pan.

'Better watch this, Chris,' he said. 'Your turn tomorrow mornin'.'

As they finished breakfast they heard a dog bark and going to the door they saw Willie arriving on his horse followed by his three cattle dogs, who, after an exploratory sniff, all lifted their legs in turn on the chopping block. One jumped up on Ernie and tried to lick his face. Ernie wasn't having any of that and said, 'Get down, yer mangy cur. When I want to wash me face I'll use water.'

Getting down from his horse and telling his dogs to get in behind, Willie said, 'G'day. Nice day, eh? Are youse goin' up the hill this mornin' after I've shown yer the track?'

'Don't think so,' replied Ernie. 'We'll go tomorrer. We'll 'ave another crack up the flats. I reckon we'll leave earlier and go further up. I want to make some bread and young Chris doesn't know it yet but he's goin' to make a stew.'

'Yeah, should be jake,' said Willie. 'Weather looks good for a few more days. Bloke reckoned on the forecast last night that there's rain comin' in about three days – not that them fellers know much about it. Reckon me old rheumatics are the best forecast. If yer ready, I'll show yer the track.'

Ernie and Chris followed him along the track. The dogs kept busy investigating interesting smells in the grass and fern along the way. Every now and again one would lift his leg and mark the territory. At one stage they found and chased an opossum that was a bit late getting home after a night's feeding. It beat them to the trees and scuttled up the trunk of a small rimu where it sat and eyed the dogs with contempt. They barked and leapt at the base of the tree but the opossum was quite safe. Old Willie yelled at them, 'Get in behind, yer lousy curs!' Two of the dogs left the tree but the third continued barking.

'I'll come and sort yer out, Glen,' shouted Willie, and he picked up a stick and advanced on Glen. The dog, seeing the stick, realised the boss meant business and after a couple of barks as a parting shot, left the tree and slunk in behind.

'Bloody dogs,' said Willie. 'Can never leave them 'possums alone. They never catch one, so why they bother, I don't know.'

Peace restored, they continued on along the track until they reached a little stream from which they drew their water.

'Here's where yer turn off,' said Willie. 'Yer just follow this faint track upstream for about four hundred yards, then you'll see where it zigzags up on to the ridge. It's easier to see from where it turns off. Once you're on top of the ridge she's plain sailin' right to the top. About halfway up, just before yer run out of the bush, the ridge flattens out, like, and there's a small tarn in a clearin' in the bush.

'The creek starts there. A few deer often drink from the tarn mornin' and evenin'. You'll know when yer get near it. There's an old dead rimu tree beside the track. Struck by lightnin', she was, about ten years ago. Now, if youse jokers are all set, I'll 'ave to be goin'. The trucks comin' for the cattle this mornin' to take them to the Ranginui Sale and I want to be there, otherwise old Ned might send the wrong ones.'

'Thanks, Willie,' said Ernie. 'Me and Chris will be okay now. We'll go down with yer as far as the hut to get our rifles and packs then we'll go and 'ave a shufti at this tarn, like, and see if there's anything there. Probably a bit late, but yer never know; and the exercise will do the boy good.'

'Aw yer might be lucky, mate,' said Willie. 'Last time I was up there I saw four deer drinkin' at midday. Reckon they see so few people up there they've got cheeky.'

After collecting their rifles and packs, Ernie and Chris retraced their steps to where the track branched off up the creek. They found the spot where the track left the stream and sidled up through the zigzag to the top of the ridge. It was quite well-formed but fairly steep and it soon started to tax Ernie's strength; he realised that he wasn't exactly in peak condition.

'All that stale beer,' he said to himself. 'Young Chris seems to be okay. Reckon the young bugger probably belonged to one of them fitness clubs in the city. Aw well, a few days and a bloke'll be as good as gold.' He mopped the sweat from his brow with the back of his hand and said to Chris, ''Struth, mate. She's bloody steep, is this 'ere track.'

'It certainly is,' agreed Chris. 'Very strenuous indeed.' He was also perspiring freely in spite of the track being shaded by the thick bush.

'A real bastard, boy,' said Ernie.

'Yes, I would have to agree with you, Ernie. It is a real bastard,' said Chris with a twinkle in his eye. 'Maybe if we had a wee spell and a mug of tea out of a flask it wouldn't be such a bastard.'

'Yeah a good idea, Chris,' Ernie said. 'If we had a flask, like.'

'How about his then? said Chris, producing the flask from his pack like a rabbit from a hat. 'I filled it up this morning while you were outside.' He unscrewed the top and poured the tea into two mugs, which he had also produced from his pack, and passed one to Ernie. 'Get that into you, mate. I'm sorry there's no sugar. I forgot that.'

'Well stone the crows, boy, yer learn fast, I'll say that for yer,' said Ernie. 'Don't worry about the sugar. The tea's the caper.'

Ernie could hardly believe the change in Chris: since he had shot his first deer he seemed to have gained so much confidence. Not that he didn't have confidence when they first met, but it was the wrong sort of confidence. Noticed he didn't shave this mornin' either, he mused, perhaps he's goin' to grow a beard like me. That would be a bit of a dag. Bet his old woman would go crook if she knew.

They finished their tea and stood up again, feeling much refreshed after the spell and the drink. Picking up their rifles and packs, they attacked the climb again and found it much easier after the rest. Two friendly little fantails kept pace with them, flitting from bough to bough in the trees beside the track. A big fat native pigeon took fright and flew off into the safety of the bush. They soon gained the top of the ridge where the track swung to the right and carried on to the country above the bushline. The grade was now much easier and they were able to proceed at a faster pace.

'After we've been up here a few times we should be pretty fit, Ernie,' said Chris.

'That's right mate,' agreed Ernie. 'Anyway it's much easier goin' now'.

Not long after that they reached the dead rimu. Ernie stopped and said in a low voice, 'That's the dead tree that old Willie was talkin' about. We can't be far from the tarn now, so I reckon we should go quiet, like.'

He unslung his rifle and, working the bolt to put a round into the chamber, he continued, 'Best be ready, boy. If there's anything there we'll 'ave to shoot real quick 'cos they'll be back into the bush quicker than a rat back into its hole.'

With their rifles ready they sneaked along the track. Suddenly there was the tarn in front of them, the water clear, cool and still in the mountain air. Ferns grew round the edge, their fronds trailing in the water. No wind ruffled the surface which reflected the surrounding trees in its mirror-like water. In a photograph it would have been difficult to ascertain what was real and what was reflection. Chris felt humbled at the scene; that nature could produce something so flawless. All this was digested in a fraction of a second, because at the far end of the pond there was a twelve-pointer stag, drinking peacefully from the pond.

Both men raised their rifles and their two shots rang out almost together. The stag dropped where he stood and lay still. Some wild ducks, who had been feeding amongst the fern around the edge of the tarn, took wing and flew, quacking in indignation at being disturbed, towards the distant river flats.

'C'mon, Chris,' said Ernie. 'We'll go and get his tail. Real team effort that one, eh?'

'Yes,' agreed Chris 'Neither of us will be able to take credit for that one.'

They pushed their way through the thick fern that grew at the tarn's edge, to the far end. Ernie took out his knife and neatly severed the tail.

'Ha, look at that, boy,' he said. 'Two hits within cooee of each other, so we both got the bugger. Real beaut head too. See how even the points are. Be worth a few bob mounted. Some city slicker would sell his own grandmother to have that mounted on his office wall so he could boast about it at the office party. Aw well, we've just got to leave it 'ere. C'mon we'll go back down the hill and I'll make some bread while you cut up the stew to take with us up the hill tomorrow. Later on we'll go up river again. If we get away straight after lunch we can get a good afternoon in.'

'Are we coming up here again tomorrow, Ernie? asked Chris.

'Yeah, I reckon,' answered Ernie. 'While the weather's good. Yer don't want to be on them tops when she's rainin' or snowin', like. Gets real brass monkeyish when she's wet up there and Willie reckoned we've only got a few fine days left before the next storm, so if we leave early tomorrer mornin', we can shoot up there for a couple of days. Right, c'mon then. Let's get crackin'.'

It was so easy coming down off the hill; Chris could hardly believe it when they reached the creek. From there it was only a short distance to the hut.

'Right,' said Ernie. 'We'll 'ave a brew and a bite to eat. Then I'll make me bread while you cut up the meat for the stew. We'll throw in some carrots and onions and leave it to cook slowly while we're upriver. We'll 'ave quite a load to take up tomorrer. That tent fly's pretty heavy. Will a tin of beans do yer for lunch?'

'Yes, that will do fine,' answered Chris. He grabbed a tin of baked beans off the shelf and, taking the tin opener, worked on the tin as he had seen Ernie do with the jam. Then he looked at the tin with a lost look on his face. Ernie took out a small pan and said, 'Empty the beans into that and put it on the fire; and keep stirrin' it so it don't catch on the bottom. Fire needs a bit of a poke and some wood too.'

Ernie put the billy on to boil for tea and set out the plates on the table. Good to see the boy pullin' his weight, he thought. He was really starting to get the hang of things – looked like he might be lucky with his companion after all. He picked things up quickly and was a real sniper with the rifle. He'd have done well in the army, being able to shoot like that: young bugger would have been an officer with all his education and upbringing. Aw well, even they were necessary, he supposed. Anyway, the young blighter was lucky he missed it. There was no glory in it; only a lot of suffering and discomfort.

After a while, Chris said, 'I reckon those beans are hot enough now. Shall I dish them up?'

'Yeah, matey, you do that,' said Ernie.

After lunch, during which they cleaned up the last of their bread, Ernie got out the ingredients for baking while Chris went out to the tree at the back of the hut and came back with one of the legs of venison.

Ernie said, 'Okay lad, this is what yer do. Cut it up into small pieces like this. Yer might find some bits of sackin' stickin' to the meat, but that won't 'urt none – just scrape it off. Then cut up some carrots and onions and mix 'em with the meat. Bit o' salt, and there's yer stew. We'll leave it to cook while we're away this afternoon. 'Avin' the early lunch means we'll be able to get a good way up the river.'

He mixed up the ingredients for his bread, added yeast, draped a cloth over it, and put it on the window sill in the sun to rise.

Later, when they returned from the afternoon shoot, he would put it in the camp oven and cook it in the embers of the fire.

'Where did you learn to cook, Ernie? asked Chris.

Ernie looked at Chris and said, 'Would yer believe that when I first joined up in 1939, they put me on a cookin' course? Thought they was goin' to make a cook out of me – I soon changed their ideas. Made so many failures the captain reckoned I'd poison the whole New Zealand Army so they transferred me to the infantry. I learnt a lot, though, in the short time I was on the course. 'Ave yer got that stew finished yet? If so, put 'er on the fire and we'll away. Should be ready when we get back. Got yer gun and pack?'

'Yes,' replied Chris. 'And I filled the flask again.'

'Good on yer, mate,' said Ernie.

They set off up the track, Chris still marvelling at the beauty of the scene laid out before him. No doubt it looked different in the wet, but days like this surely made up for any discomfort experienced at those times. He was sure that he was coming to love this country. Never did he think that he, a city boy, would be happy in such isolation. He was already forgetting about electric light, television and all the other so-called advantages of city life. Yes, even his pride and joy, the MG sports car bestowed on him by a doting mother on his twenty-first birthday. Why, he hadn't even bothered to switch on the transistor radio or started to read any of the paperbacks he had brought with him. The days seemed to go so fast.

However, this was not the time for dreaming. This was the time when he had to concentrate on what Ernie had told him. Watch where you put your feet, keep quiet, and continually scan the country for signs of deer. They crossed the little stream, which Chris, on the spur of the moment, had christened Katie's Creek after the 'washing' episode. Chris hadn't had much to do with girls but it might have been nice if she had been seventeen instead of seventy. His mother had always been a bit of a fly in the ointment as regards girl-friends; nobody was good enough for her darling boy. He didn't think many of the city girls he knew would be much good in this environment.

'Keep yer eyes skinned, boy,' reminded Ernie, bringing Chris' thoughts back to the present.

Shortly afterwards, Chris said in a whisper, 'Over there. Six of them near the river.'

'Yeah, I see 'em,' said Ernie. Rapidly sizing up the situation, he continued, 'We'll 'ave to be careful 'ere mate, or they'll get wind of us. The afternoon breeze is blowin' in from the sea, right up the river. We'd better sneak into the bush 'ere and get level with 'em. Be much closer then.'

A few yards into the bush the going was quite good as most of the undergrowth had been stripped by the deer and opossums: the latter were becoming just as big a menace to the forest as the deer. Ernie led the way through the trees, occasionally going to the edge of the bush to check where they were in relation to their quarry.

At last he said 'Okay we're upwind of 'em now. We'll just go on a wee bit more then we can 'ave a go at 'em. The range will be about 350 yards, which is far enough; but we'll only scare 'em if we try to get closer.'

After another hundred yards Ernie turned toward the edge of the bush. They stopped just before the first line of trees to take stock of their position in relation to the deer. Sure enough, there were the deer still contentedly grazing, unaware of the close proximity of their enemies. Using tree trunks to steady their aim, they each picked out a deer and fired. Chris's animal dropped immediately but Ernie's ran for about twenty yards before stumbling and falling. Chris got another with his second shot but Ernie missed and the remaining three escaped across the river.

'Good shootin', lad,' said Ernie. 'C'mon, we'll get their tails and then go on up the river. Shows they haven't been disturbed much to see them out this early in the afternoon.'

Tails collected, they continued on their way upstream. After some distance, a ridge ran out from the hills on side of the river, effectively cutting the flats in two. Thick bush grew on these ridges, which ended in bluffs at the water's edge. The bluffs made a short gorge through which the river flowed swift and deep, so the only way to continue was to scramble over a bluff.

'What do yer reckon?' asked Ernie. 'Shall we give it a go now?'

'Might as well,' replied Chris. 'It's early and our shots won't have been heard by any deer on the other side of the ridge. I reckon there's a track up through the trees over there. That should take us to the top.'

'Okay yer keen young bugger, c'mon then,' grinned Ernie. 'You take the lead and don't go too bloomin' fast.'

Chris set off, followed by Ernie. It was amazing how he had come to accept Chris as an equal: until recently he wouldn't have even bothered to ask Chris' opinion and now here he was following along behind.

The track wound its way up the side of the ridge. The grade

was relatively easy but the surface was very uneven, with large roots sticking up to trip the unwary. At the top of the ridge there was a small clearing with a large outcrop of rock in it. Beyond the clearing the track continued down the other side of the ridge where grade became much steeper and the muddy surface made progress treacherous. Here, tree roots protruded from the mud and low-hanging branches waited their turn to impede progress.

'Be a bastard gettin' back up again,' said Ernie, as he fell in the mud for the third time.

'Yes, it will,' agreed Chris 'A fair bastard.'

Ernie couldn't help but grin at Chris's use of the word bastard – this was the second time he had used it. Ernie was sure he had never used such language before he took up hunting. Just imagine what old mum would have to say about it!

Finally, after much slipping and sliding, the two men arrived at the bottom of the ridge. Ernie, who had resumed the lead as they left the ridge, raised his hand and they stopped just inside the trees. There, on a large grassy flat, bordered by the river on one side and the bushclad slopes on the other, was a mob of twenty deer. Two stags, one older than the other, were shaping up to each other in the middle of the flat and the hinds were standing around to see who won the inevitable fight.

'Hey, look at that, Ernie,' whispered Chris. 'Look at those two stags. They look as though they are going to fight.'

'Yeah,' agreed Ernie. He unslung his rifle and continued, 'In the wild, the buggers will fight each other at the drop of a hat to see who gets the girls. Yer see, it's a bit like people; the young jokers are always tryin' to throw their weight about with the old blokes. If the old stag wins, he gets the prize: the young one wins, he gets 'em and the old feller will go and try his luck elsewhere. While they're busy there they're not worryin' about us. Okay, rapid fire and we'll drop as many as we can.'

The shooting was almost a massacre. After the first shots the deer milled around in complete disarray, not knowing where death was coming from. The two stags broke off their combat, the old one falling dead from the hail of bullets. Finally about six deer, including the young stag, made for the river, plunged in, and swam to the safety of the other side.

'Whew,' said Ernie. 'That was shootin', that was. Yer did good, young Chris.'

'Thanks,' said Chris, 'but I do feel sad, having shot those lovely animals.'

'Yeah, I know 'ow yer feel,' said Ernie as he reloaded his magazine, 'but look at it this way: if them deer are allowed to increase much more we won't 'ave all this beaut bush around and the erosion will get worse. Then the rivers will flood more often and ruin the farmland and flood the cities and towns. So yer see it's necessary to shoot the blighters.'

'Yes, I see your point, Ernie. I guess it's something we've just got to do. The main thing is to make a clean job of it and not leave any to die of their wounds in agony. Shall we collect the tails now? Shall I cut out a couple of steaks for tea?'

'Real tiger for yer steaks, ain't yer?' laughed Ernie. 'Yeah, you do that, boy. We'll 'ave steak instead of stew, if yer like. The stew'll keep.'

They were about halfway through collecting the tails when they heard the sound of a light aircraft flying up the river. The engine appeared to be running rather roughly and, just as the plane came out of the gorge its engine stopped altogether and it swung around toward the clearing.

Weaving from side to side, it crossed the clearing and, narrowly missing the men, crashed into the trees with much rending and tearing of metal. There was a sudden silence and for a few moments they were rooted to the spot. Ernie was the first one to realise what had happened and, yelling to Chris to 'c'mon', he ran across the clearing to the wreck, which was just inside the trees. The impact had torn the wings off and the fuselage had skidded a few yards further. Fortunately it had not struck the trunks of the trees but had come to rest between two of them. It was not as badly damaged as it may have been, the undergrowth having cushioned the impact.

When they got to the plane, they could see two figures sitting side by side in the wrecked cockpit. The pilot was slumped forward in his safety harness in the left seat. His face was covered with blood from where it had made contact with the buckled windscreen surround. The passenger was still sitting upright and, as the two men approached, she turned her head toward them with a pleading look in her eyes.

Chris climbed up on the three foot section of the right wing still attached to the fuselage. He pulled at the door but it was stuck fast. 'Look, mate,' said Ernie. 'There's a sign on a panel to yer left that says 'axe' – see if yer can open it.'

Chris punched at the catch on the panel and, sure enough, there was a small axe in the compartment. Ripping it out, he attacked the door and after a few blows succeeded in tearing it from its fastenings. He undid the girl's seat-belt and said, 'We'll soon have you out of there.' He gently lifted her and slid her out on what remained of the wing. She groaned and he asked, 'Can you speak? If so, please tell me where you hurt.'

In a faint voice, the girl said, 'It's my left arm and chest. How's my brother? Please get him out.'

'We will,' Chris assured her. 'We'll carry you away from the plane and then we'll get him out.'

Between them they helped her to a safe distance from the plane. Chris took off his jacket and spread it on the ground and they laid her gently on top of it.

'You stay with her, Ernie,' suggested Chris, 'and I'll have a go at getting the pilot out. I'll see if I can find a first aid kit, too.'

Hurrying back to the aircraft, he picked up the axe and climbed onto the left wing: there was about five feet left reasonably intact which made for easier working. He struck at the door with the axe and succeeded in removing it. He undid the pilot's harness and looked to see if he could detect any signs of life. There appeared to be a faint pulse in the neck and the eyes flickered open briefly.

'I'd better have some assistance, please Ernie,' he called.

'Will yer be okay, miss?' asked Ernie. 'Me mate wants a hand. I'll be back in a minute.'

He hurried over to the plane and clambered up onto the wing beside Chris, ''Ow is he?' he asked.

'He doesn't look too good,' replied Chris, 'and it looks as though his right foot is caught under the rudder bar. Can you watch him while I go round the other side and try to lever the rudder bar up with the axe handle? There's an awful smell of petrol, so we'll have to hurry.'

Chris jumped off the wing and ran round to the other side of the plane. Climbing into the copilot's seat, he pushed the axe handle down under the bent rudder bar and levered upwards, praying that it wouldn't break under the strain because it was all they had. One of their rifles would have been strong enough but it would probably have been too long to fit in the confined space. Besides, in their hurry to get to the wreck, they had left their rifles and packs out on the flat with the deer. What with the strong smell of petrol and the hot engine, time was most important.

Fortunately the axe handle proved strong enough and Chris felt the rudder bar move. Throwing the axe aside, he gently grasped the pilot's leg and pulled it free.

'Okay Ernie,' he said. 'His leg is free now. I'll come round your side and we'll get him out. Ah, here's the first aid kit. I'll bring that with me.'

Between the two of them they managed to get the pilot out of his seat and through the door. At one stage he came round and let out a cry and then relapsed into unconsciousness again.

'He's so badly hurt, it's just as well he's out of it, even though they say you're not supposed to move a badly injured person. But with the danger of fire we didn't have much option,' said Chris.

'Yeah,' agreed Ernie. 'We'd better get 'im over beside the girl and see what we can do for 'em. I'll 'ave to try and remember me army first aid trainin'.'

They carried him over to his companion and tried to make them comfortable. It appeared that the girl had a fractured left arm and bruising on the chest from the safety harness. The pilot was more badly injured and there was little they could do, other than keep him warm. Ernie went over and picked up their packs and they wrapped the parkas and leggings plus their packs round the victims as best they could.

'I know they reckon you shouldn't move an injured person unless you know it is safe to do so but, in this case, we had little alternative,' said Chris. 'Look Ernie, no offence, but I'm a lot fitter than you. You stay here and look after these two and I'll go for assistance. If I really hurry I can get to Hobson's place and ring the police and, hopefully, get a helicopter in here before dark. There's no way they could get a stretcher up that muddy track. It's lucky the plane didn't burn: if it was going to it would have gone up by now. All right Ernie, I'll see you later.'

It was fortunate that Chris was fairly fit – he almost ran up the muddy track to the top of the ridge. He grasped at tree roots and branches to haul himself up. In some ways it was easier going up than down as he didn't have the fear of falling on his face. Gaining the top he had a minute's breather and then set off down the other side. When he reached the flat he broke into a steady trot and was thankful for the run he had done every morning before he took up deer culling. He kept up a steady mile-consuming pace along the track, looking neither right nor left but keeping his eyes on where he was going. He passed the turn-off to the hut and wondered how the stew was doing; probably cooked nicely by now. It was a good thing the fire would be dying down so it wouldn't come to any harm. Whether they would ever get to eating it or the steaks tonight was anybody's guess. He ran through the bush to the gate at the end of the road. He climbed over it and ran on and soon came to the gate into the Hobson property. He ran up the drive and knocked loudly on the door, which was opened by old Katie.

'Well! well!' she exclaimed, 'if it's not my boy who likes to bathe in his birthday suit. Yer don't look so interesting in yer clothes. What can an old girl like me do yer for? Hey – you look completely buggered. What on earth 'ave yer been doing?'

'I am,' confessed Chris. 'I've just run all the way from the other side of the big bluff up the river. A light plane has crashed up there. Ernie and I pulled the pilot and his passenger out of the wreckage. They're badly hurt – especially the pilot. Can I ring the police from here, please? They'll need a helicopter to get them out.'

'C'mon in, boy,' said Katie, grasping his arm and dragging him inside. 'There's the phone on the wall over there. You ring the cops. One long ring gets the exchange. Hope there's no gossiping old biddies on the line: if there is, let me know and I'll shift 'em. I'll make yer a cuppa tea while yer doin' that.'

Chris lifted the receiver, found the line clear and gave one long ring. The girl in the exchange said: 'Number please,' and he asked to be put through to the police. In a few moments a voice said, 'Ranginui Police. Constable Walker speaking. How can I help?'

Chris quickly told the constable his name, where he was ringing from and what had occurred. The policeman said, 'We've just had word that there's a light plane overdue. There's a helicopter warming up at the aerodrome now to go and search. Hang on a moment, will you?'

Chris could hear the policeman talking to somebody on a radio-telephone – probably the pilot of the chopper. The constable came back on the line and said, 'Are you there, sir? The chopper will pick you up at Hobson's farm in a few minutes. They're just about to take off and they have a doctor on board. Please go with them and show the pilot where to go.'

'Okay constable,' said Chris. He replaced the receiver and said to Katie, 'They're picking me up in a few minutes. Where do you think they will land?'

'Oh, in the front paddock there, I reckon,' she replied. 'Only paddock that hasn't got stumps and logs in it. Me brothers never get round to clearin' any of the rest of the farm. 'Ere, you'd better get this mug of tea inside yer before yer go ridin' in that helicopter. And here's a couple of scones, too.'

'Gosh, thanks ma'am,' said Chris. 'That is very kind of you.'

'What's this ma'am caper?' said Katie. 'Me mates call me Katie.'

Chris swallowed down the strong hot tea, feeling strength return to his limbs after the long run. Gathering up the scones, he left the kitchen and with a wave to Katie, hurried out to the paddock.

'My word,' he thought. 'Katie certainly makes good scones. Bit of an old character really, but, like Ernie, if you can break through that hard crust, you'll find a heart of gold underneath.'

Chris was just starting to find out what West Coast hospitality and neighbourly care was all about. By the time he reached the paddock and climbed through the barbed wire fence, ripping his trousers as he did so, he could hear the beat of the helicopter's rotors in the distance. It soon appeared, flying up the river. Opposite the Hobson's house it turned and flew in towards the paddock where it settled down close to where Chris was standing. The pilot opened the door and beckoned Chris forward. Keeping his head bent, as he had seen people do on television when approaching a helicopter, he went across to the machine and climbed in beside the pilot. It was the first time he had been in a chopper and he was quite looking forward to the experience; although it was a pity it was not under happier circumstances. The pilot showed him how to fasten his seat-belt. Two other men, one a policeman in uniform, sat in the rear seat. Two stretchers were fastened on to the skids on the outside of the aircraft. The pilot passed Chris a set of earphones with a mike attached, which he put on.

The pilot said, 'Can you hear me okay?' and, on getting Chris' affirmative reply, continued. 'Right, here we go.' The machine lifted off and headed back toward the river. Old Katie was out on the lawn, waving as they flew away.

'My name's Andrew Lucas,' said the pilot. 'Now, where do we go?'

Chris replied 'I'm Christopher. Just fly straight upstream until we come to the first gorge. Just through the gorge and on a flat to the left is where the wreck is – it's not far, fortunately.'

'All right,' said the pilot. 'Did you run down from up there? It didn't seem long from when we got word that the plane was missing to when you phoned up.'

'Yes I did,' replied Chris. 'But it's much easier going this way.'

'I bet,' said Andrew. 'Here's the gorge coming up'.

After flying through the gorge, he swung the helicopter round to the left and said, 'It looks okay to land on that grassy flat. Hell! who shot all those deer?'

'My mate Ernie and I,' said Chris. 'We're deer cullers.'

Andrew skilfully brought the chopper in to a smooth landing very close to where Ernie was waiting beside the two patients.

CHAPTER NINE

Ernie had settled himself into what he expected would be a long wait. After all, he reckoned Chris had a long way to run and, by the time he got through to the police and they organised a search aircraft, it would be a miracle if anyone arrived much before dark. He hoped he wasn't going to have to spend the night up here with the victims of the accident because, while the girl wasn't so bad, except for a lot of pain in her broken arm, he doubted whether the pilot would be alive come morning. There was little he could do for the poor chap except try to keep him warm.

The girl told Ernie her name was Mary Thomas and her companion was her brother, James. He had been a pilot for some time and they were on a short flight to test the engine. She didn't know what had gone wrong but, soon after they had passed the Hobson farm the motor had missed a couple of times then seemed to pick up all right and they had carried on, intending to fly through the gorge and then return to Ranginui. She worked in a local solicitor's office. Ernie could see that under normal circumstances she would be a very attractive-looking girl. He was able to give her some hot tea from the flask in his pack, which cheered her up a bit.

He told her how Chris had gone for help, but didn't let on to her that they might be marooned there all night.

Ernie was most surprised, therefore, when he detected the sound of a helicopter. Within a few minutes it appeared from out of the gorge, swung round toward the flat and came in to land close by. The pilot cut the motor and climbed out with three others – one of whom was Chris. Ernie dashed out to meet them and said, ''Struth, I didn't expect youse jokers so soon. Yer must 'ave run fast, young Chris.'

'Well, Ernie,' said Chris, 'I guess I was lucky. Everything seemed to go right. When I rang the police they already had the chopper ready to go. You see, the plane had just been reported missing. It was only supposed to be a fifteen minute flight. Engine test or something.'

'Yeah, so the girl said,' Ernie replied. 'So yer hitched a ride back.'

'They wanted me to show them where you were.'

By then, the doctor, who was the other passenger, was examining the two patients and the policeman and the pilot were unfastening the stretchers from the helicopter. They called to Ernie and Chris to give them a hand to carry the stretchers over to where Mary and her brother were lying. The doctor stood up from his examination and said, 'Not much we can do here – hospital as soon as possible for both of them. Come on, we'll get them on the stretchers and then we'll go.' To the policeman, he said, 'Do you want to have a look at the wreck, Mark? If not, I would prefer to be on the way.'

'No, Doc,' replied the policeman. 'That can wait. The Inspector of Air Accidents will have to be informed. I expect he will be here tomorrow. Probably another job for Andrew to fly him in.'

The stretchers loaded, Andrew said, 'All aboard. There's room for you and your mate, Chris, if you want to come. I could drop you off at Hobson's farm. Would that be okay, doc? It's on our way and will only take a minute.'

'As long as the stop is only brief,' replied the doctor. 'I want to get these folk to hospital without too much delay. But it'll be all right.'

'Do you want to go, Chris?' asked Andrew.

'Yes,' Chris answered. 'We'll go, won't we, Ernie?'

'Yeah, I suppose so,' said Ernie. 'I don't hold with them things.'

Ernie didn't look too happy at the prospect of his first flight, but it was a hell of a climb over that bluff and he was getting a bit tired. It had been quite a day.

Once they were all in the helicopter and belted up the pilot started the engine and they were soon airborne and heading down the river. It was only a short flight back to the Hobson's farm and Andrew made the brief stop to let Chris and Ernie out. The policeman called out that he would require a statement from them on what had happened. The chopper lifted off again and continued on its way to town and hospital for Mary and James.

'How did you like that, Ernie?' asked Chris knowing full well what the answer would be. He had seen the look of fear on Ernie's face during the flight.

'Bloody scary, mate,' replied Ernie. 'I'm still shakin'. Yer won't get me back in one of them things again, not for anythin'.'

'Oh go on, Ernie,' teased Chris. 'It was fun. I wouldn't mind learning to fly a helicopter.' Changing the subject, he continued 'Do you realise that we've left our packs and rifles upriver? We'll have to go back for them tomorrow instead of going up the hill. We've got to collect the tails, too.'

'Aw cripes,' grumbled Ernie. 'That means we've got to go over that flamin' muddy track again.'

'I'm afraid so,' said Chris. 'Never mind. Think of that stew for tea.'

'A few beers would be better,' said Ernie. 'I've got a thirst like a camel.'

By this time they had reached the Hobson house to be greeted by Katie and Willie.

'Ha, the heroes return,' called Katie. 'You boys will be wantin' a beer after all that, eh? C'mon in and tell us all about it'.

Okay, said Ernie enthusiastically, ready, as always, to accept an invitation to a few beers.

They followed Willie and Katie into the big farm kitchen. Seated in an old leather armchair to one side of the big wood range was an old bald-headed man with what could only be described as a walrus moustache. He wore an old patched khaki shirt and battledress trousers, which were stuffed into gumboots. Clouds of pungent smoke floated around him from an old battered bent-stem pipe which was firmly clamped in his jaws. On his head was an old tank corps beret. A big black cat sat on his knee and its purring could be distinctly heard above the sound of an old radio that occupied a small table in the corner of the room.

'This is me brother, Ned,' said Willie. 'Ned, these are the blokes what rescued them folk from the aeroplane up the river; Ernie and Chris. They're the deer cullers from up at the hut. I've brought 'em in for a beer.'

Old Ned staggered to his feet, upsetting the black cat, who complained bitterly as he did so. He thrust out a hand as big as a dinner plate and said, 'Pleased to meet yer. I'll get the beer.' He stumbled off through a door on the other side of the range and emerged a few moments later carrying a crate of beer. 'There yer are,' he said. 'Get into it.'

'I say,' said Chris quite taken aback by so much beer. 'We can't stay drinking all night, you know. We've got to get up early tomorrow morning to go back upriver to collect our rifles.'

'Ain't all for you, young feller,' said Ned, plonking the crate down on the table with enough force to make the dishes rattle. 'There's only a dozen there and there's four of us. That's three each. Soon get them under our belts. Katie, 'ere, she don't drink much beer. She'll 'ave a gin and tonic – won't yer, girl?'

Chris could see he was going to have a bit of a problem. While he could drink one or even two glasses on occasions, there was no way that he could keep up with these people. Obviously they would have a certain contempt for someone as abstemious as him *and* he didn't want to have to carry Ernie home. Little did he know that it would take a lot more than three bottles to put Ernie out for the count.

'Just a glass for me, please,' he said in a meek voice.

'What do yer mean a glass, boy?' snorted Ned. 'Yer drink out of the bottle 'ere like the rest of us, or yer don't drink at all. Now get that into yer,' and he passed a bottle to Chris, who took a tentative sip at it.

'Go on, down the hatch, mate,' said Ned, contempt in his voice.

'Look,' said Chris. 'I don't want to offend but really I don't drink much.'

'Gawd!' exclaimed Ned in disgust. 'If there's one thing I can't stand it's a flamin' piker.'

'You leave him alone,' said Katie. 'If the boy doesn't want to drink, leave 'im be. At least he could teach you a lesson, yer old soak. Don't take any notice of him, lad.'

In the meantime, Willie had opened a couple of bottles and he and Ernie were well on their way to getting through their first ones.

'Gee that's good,' said Ernie, smacking his lips and taking another long swig at his bottle. 'That's the trouble with deer cullin', like. Yer can't duck into the pub when yer feel like it.'

Katie poured herself a generous gin and tonic. Generous on the gin and not much tonic. She said to Chris, 'Leave them boozy bastards and come over here and tell an old woman about what happened up the river.' She sat down on an old *chaise longue* that was losing its stuffing, and patted the space beside her.

He went over and sat down and told her all about the afternoon's adventure. The other three spent the time making inroads into the crate of beer. Katie passed Chris a glass and said, 'Use that lad. Yer don't look very comfortable drinkin' out of the bottle. Do yer mean to tell me you ran all the way here from the other side of the gorge?'

'Most of the way,' replied Chris.

'More than those old soaks could do,' she said. 'If they had the trots they wouldn't be able to run to the dunny. I reckon yer deserve a medal, boy.'

'Oh, it was nothing,' said Chris. 'I just happened to be the fitter of the two of us and Ernie stayed behind and looked after the couple while I was away. All I hope is that they are all right.'

'Well if they are, it's thanks to you, lad,' said Katie.

Old Ned took his bottle away from his mouth long enough to say, 'Yer can't trust them flyin' machines. Drop yer in it every time.'

Chris was wondering how much longer he would have to spend at the Hobson's place. No doubt they meant well and in their funny way considered themselves hospitable. Ernie looked set for a long session and, try as he might, Chris could see no way out of the situation.

'I'll go and get some more beer,' announced Ned. 'Youse jokers look like yer still thirsty. What about you, boy? Yer not drinkin' out of a glass, are yer?' He went over to the door and disappeared once more into the room beside the stove only to come back in a few moments with a look of disgust on his craggy old face. 'There's no more bloody beer,' he said. 'Cripes, a man'll die of thirst round this place. Who's the dopey bastard what forgot to stock up in town the other day?'

'Well, you were the one that went to town,' Katie pointed out. 'Why didn't you buy some more? Anyway, yer not supposed to be drivin'. 'Ave yer forgotten they took yer licence off of yer for bein' drunk in charge a coupla months ago?'

Chris saw his chance. He got up and said, 'C'mon, Ernie. It's time we went back to the hut. We don't want that stew to burn.'

Once the beer was cut, old Ernie was quite happy about going – especially for a feed of stew. After all, in his world, food was the most important thing next to beer.

'Yeah,' he agreed. 'Better get goin'. Thanks, youse jokers. As the boy says, we don't want that stew to burn. Well, hooray then.'

He hurried out of the door and down the drive like the devil himself was after him. Chris said a hurried farewell to the trio and followed close behind Ernie, hardly able to believe his good fortune. He shuddered to think what time they would have got away if Ned had found more beer. Willie and Katie were all right but that old Ned was certainly a queer fish.

'Hey,' shouted Willie. 'You'd better take this torch, like. She gets as dark as the inside of a cow in the bush at night. Wouldn't want yer havin' an accident. Might 'ave to get that there helicopter out again. Hah, hah, hah!'

Chris took the torch said 'Thanks Willie. Good night,' and hurried after Ernie. He didn't want to get caught up with the Hobsons again.

They arrived back at the hut to find the fire almost out. However, the application of some twigs and small wood, together with some beery blowing from Ernie, soon had it blazing again and it was not long before the stew was reheated and filling the hut with a appetising aroma. Chris took plates, knives and forks from the shelf and said, 'That smells good.'

'Yeah,' agreed Ernie. 'Yer can't beat venison stew, boy. C'mon, pass yer plate and I'll dish it up.'

Chris took his first mouthful and said, 'My word, it *is* good. You wouldn't get better in a city restaurant.'

'Ain't never been in one of them places,' said Ernie. 'Had a few bar meals in the pub, though.'

The meal finished Chris put on a billy of water for a brew of tea and to wash the dishes. Chris liked to wash the dishes, then he knew it was done properly. Ernie wasn't overly fussy in that field.

'I reckon I'll hit the sack early tonight, lad,' he said. 'Must be gettin' old. Can't take it like I used to. Gotta get up the river for them rifles in the mornin', too. We should 'ave brought them back in the chopper with us. Be just our luck to see a swag of deer on the way up and no guns. Holy smoke, I forgot me bread!' He jumped to his feet and rushed over to the window sill. He lifted the cloth and said, 'She's risen good. I'll put it in the camp oven and see 'ow she goes. 'Ope it wasn't sittin' there too long.' He took the camp oven out from under the bench, looked inside, tipped out a few dead leaves and some dust. He placed the dough in the oven, buried it in the embers, heaped more on top and said, 'We'll see 'ow she is in the mornin'.'

Next morning after breakfast, which included some of Ernie's bread, they set off upriver again. Contrary to Ernie's prediction no deer were sighted but the usual paradise ducks started squawking and flew away off to the river. Chris presumed they were the ones they saw each time they came up the river. They negotiated the muddy track, helped, no doubt, by Ernie's lurid comments on the condition of it and the ancestry of whoever constructed it. It was difficult to believe as they gazed over the flat that such a drama had taken place there the day before, but the sight of the wrecked aeroplane lying in the trees was solid evidence of the event.

''Struth, them youngsters were lucky,' said Ernie.

'Yes, they certainly were,' agreed Chris. 'Well, we'd better get those tails, I suppose, and get back downriver. You've got to climb over that track again, Ernie. Pity the chopper isn't here.'

'What!' exclaimed Ernie. 'Ride in that rowdy bastard again. Not bloody likely. I'll walk thanks, mate, muddy track or no muddy track. A man can trust his feet better than them helicopters.'

It didn't take them long to gather up the tails and their gear. They then set off for the hut, Chris leading the way. Ernie once again told the track what he thought of it. Chris was sure Ernie believed the track understood what he said, but it didn't appear to make the climb any easier.

'A few more times up this track and you'll be running over it,' joked Chris.

'Huh,' grunted Ernie as he stumbled over a root.

When they arrived back at the hut it was still quite early. Chris suggested they have a snack and a cup of tea and then set off for the top of the hill.

'Yeah, guess we could,' agreed Ernie, sounding a bit doubtful about it 'Gotta clean yer rifle first though. Gotta look after yer gun, lad.'

'Don't you like the idea of the climb, Ernie?'

'Aw, it's just that this joker's so unfit, like, but I suppose we gotta go sometime. All right, yer keen young bugger, we'll go then and if I pack it in yer'll 'ave to carry me. We'll need our sleepin' bags, that tent fly and a bit of rope to hang it over, the axe, tinned food, the billy, bread, butter, tea and all that.'

After they had cleaned their rifles and eaten, they packed up what they needed, dividing the load between them. With their rifles they were well-loaded down.

'Don't worry, Ernie,' said Chris. 'We can have plenty of spells.'

'Yeah, need 'em, mate. I'm loaded like a flamin' packhorse,' growled Ernie. 'Hey, we'd better take them ground sheets too. The ground up there will be as wet as a baby's nappy.'

Chris was amused at Ernie comparing the wet ground to a baby's nappy – fat lot of experience he would have had of those things. Neither had Chris, for that matter. Old Ernie certainly had some original sayings. Slinging their packs on their backs and shouldering their rifles, they set off for the top. Ernie puffed and blew on the zigzag and Chris was forced to stop frequently to let him recover his breath. It was becoming increasingly clear that Chris was tending to take over as leader and that Ernie was accepting it. While Ernie had more knowledge of life in the outdoors, Chris had the ability to pick things up quickly and was a natural-born leader. Maybe the confidence he displayed when they met had something to do with that.

After they gained the ridge, Ernie found the going much easier. They reached the tarn but, apart from two ducks swimming lazily across the still water, it was deserted. Chris thought it was an idyllic spot, nestled in the primeval forest: the stillness was so intense one could almost feel it. It gave him a calm, serene feeling just to be there and he wished that they could camp there for a few nights instead of higher up the hill. However, their reason for being there was to shoot deer, not admire the scenery and they really needed to be at the top to get a good start in the morning.

After the tarn they were breaking new territory and they once more plunged into an area of snow grass and scattered scrub. The surface was covered in rocks and stones with considerable areas of running shingle. Just near where the track emerged from the bush, a small stream bubbled out from a pile of rocks and chattered to itself as it hurried downhill to disappear into the bush.

'Good place to camp 'ere, Chris,' said Ernie. 'Gets the shelter of the bush and there's good water too. We can rig the rope between them two trees, sling the fly over it and peg it down. There's some dry fern too – we can spread our sleepin'-bags on. Be 'ome and 'osed 'ere, boy.'

The camp set up and the billy on to boil, the men sat down and surveyed the scene. Rugged rocky slopes interspersed with shingle slides continued to the top of the leading ridge, which went on upwards to finally join the main mountain chain in the background. There were plenty of signs of deer and the depredations caused by them: many clumps of tussock and other native vegetation had been eaten down to the ground; or worse, pulled out by the roots.

'I see what you mean by the damage the deer cause,' said Chris as he gazed about him.

'Yeah,' said Ernie. 'Y'see there's no protection from erosion on a lot of this country now. That's why we've gotta get rid of the blighters. Hey, the billy's boilin'. We'll 'ave that brew and a bit to eat and then go along the slope, eh? Might see somethin'.'

It proved to be rough going along the steep hillside and they had to follow deer tracks across the shingle slides and through the rocky outcrops. A secondary ridge came off the top and ran down to the valley floor and the river far below. The other side of this ridge, the top of which the men approached cautiously, proved to be the side of an extensive basin and an ideal habitat for deer. Sure enough, Chris' keen young eyes picked up a large mob of deer out in the middle of the basin.

'Hey, look,' he whispered. 'Do you see them up there? All round that big rock. They obviously haven't seen us.'

'Yeah, I see 'em, lad,' replied Ernie. 'Now you tell me 'ow you would tackle them fellers. See if yer've learnt anythin'.'

'Well,' said Chris. 'They haven't seen us and they haven't got wind of us, so what I suggest is that we stay below the ridge and make our way up toward the top. When we're near the top we'll be closer to them and slightly above them: you did say that it's easier shooting downhill at a target than uphill at it, didn't you?'

'Yeah, lad, I did,' answered Ernie. 'Yer learnin' good – okay, you lead the way and I'll follow.' Ernie had to admit that his companion was getting more likeable all the time. In spite of their different upbringing he was sure that they would become good mates in this deer culling job.

It was an exhausting climb along the side of the ridge. Fortunately, Ernie had sweated out most of the stale beer from the previous evening and he did not require too many spells; also, his standard of fitness was improving rapidly with all the climbing they were doing.

Finally they gained a point just below where the ridge they were following joined the main ridge. From there they looked cautiously into the basin. The deer were still there; completely oblivious to the presence of the two hunters, who were now much closer to their quarry and had the benefit of height as well.

'Okay Chris. What do yer reckon the range is?' asked Ernie as he unslung his rifle.

'About three hundred yards,' answered Chris with confidence.

'Be near enough,' said Ernie. 'You take the right and I'll go for them on the left.'

The two men lay down and fired from behind a small pile of rocks. All hell broke loose down in the basin as the deer milled around in utter confusion, having no idea where the shots were coming from. As they lived up on the high tops they were seldom disturbed and were therefore less gun-shy than the deer living further down, who tended to be much more scary. Two had fallen from the first two shots and, by the time the animals had chosen an escape route, another four had fallen to the hunters' rifles. They fled at full speed, leaping over rocks and bushes in their bid for freedom. Another one died as they cleared the ridge on the far side of the basin.

'Whew, that's seven!' exclaimed Chris.

'Yeah,' agreed Ernie, 'and the others won't stop for a while – that put the fear of the old devil himself into 'em. 'Ave to go the other way tomorrow or over to the other side of the ridge. We'll get them tails now and then go back to camp. There won't be nothin' happenin' up here for the rest of the day.'

Tails collected, they slipped and slid their way down through the shingle to their camp.

Next morning dawned with an angry looking westerly sky and a warm breeze from the nor'west.

'Some rough weather comin',' observed Ernie. 'We'll 'ave a shifty over the main ridge today. This afternoon we'll pack up and go back down the hill. Don't want to be caught up 'ere in a storm. Blow yer inside out, it would, and fair freeze yer cobblers off.'

Only two deer were shot that day, and by mid-afternoon the sky was heavy with cloud and the high peaks at the head of the river valley were completely shrouded in mist and fog.

Chris and Ernie packed up their belongings and set off down the track to the hut, not pausing on the way, as they were anxious to reach shelter before the storm broke. As they arrived the first heavy drops started to fall and soon the heavens opened and the rain came down in sheets, blown almost sideways by the strong northerly wind that howled round the hut. It was fortunate that the trees sheltered it from the worst of the wind. They got a roaring fire going and warmed up the last of the stew which, together with potatoes and carrots, made a sustaining meal.

Sitting on their bunks afterwards, drinking tea and listening to the rain hammering at the roof, they thought how lucky they were that they had come down off the mountain. Ernie rolled himself a smoke, lit up and inhaled deeply. He settled back and with a sigh of contentment, said, 'Yer know, boy, there's somethin' pretty good about sittin' 'ere, warm and dry, listenin' to the rain. She'll probably pour down all night and be a good day tomorrer. Does that on the coast, yer know. Yer get most of yer rain at night. Well, the heavy stuff anyway.'

'Yes, it's certainly raining heavily now,' said Chris. 'Bit different to the drizzle we get over the hill. If it keeps up like this all night everything will be flooded in the morning. Oh well, I think I will have a read of one of my paperbacks.'

'Look, mate,' Ernie said a bit hesitantly. 'Do yer think I could borrow one of yer books? I haven't done much readin', like, but I've always wanted to, yer know. A bloke didn't get much learnin', so 'ave yer got one without too many big words in it?'

'Yes' said Chris. 'You are most welcome. What about a Western?' He took down a few books and, sorting through them, continued, 'Here you are, Ernie. *The Range War*. It's about the Texas Rangers fighting outlaws. Give that a try.'

Ernie took the book and, reclining on his bunk, started to read, mouthing the words as he did so.

It continued to pour with rain and the wind blew with undiminished fury. The sound of the rain on the roof made conversation difficult. Ernie was so engrossed in his book that any attempt at conversation by Chris met with a grunt and at ten o'clock, when Chris announced that he was going to bed, Ernie didn't even reply.

Much later Chris was awakened by a loud peel of thunder, which he was sure was going to demolish the hut and leave them at the mercy of the storm. Ernie was lying on his back snoring lustily, the book resting on his chest. Chris quietly climbed out of his sleeping-bag, took the book from Ernie, covered him with his sleeping-bag and blew out the lamp. The rain continued its assault on the corrugated iron roof. Chris was sure that it would come right through: he had never heard anything like it. The strong wind was still howling round the hut making it shake and the flashes of lightning lit up the interior like a summer's day. He threw some more wood on the fire and heard the spatter of the raindrops as they came down the chimney and landed in the flames. How could old Ernie sleep through this infernal racket? He was thankful to climb back into his sleeping-bag again; but it was some time before he went back to sleep.

Next morning when they awoke it was still raining, although nowhere near as heavily as overnight, and the wind had dropped too.

'You must have found that a good book,' said Chris. 'You went to sleep over it, although how anyone could sleep through that racket I don't know. I was awake for quite a while after I covered you up with your sleeping-bag. I thought the hut was going to collapse.'

'Nar,' said Ernie. 'She's right, mate. That's just a normal storm 'ere. Yer want to be 'ere when she really rains. Yeah, she's a good yarn, that book. Them jokers are pretty quick on the trigger, like. I reckon I could get quite keen on that readin' caper. Well, better 'ave a dekko outside and see what she's like. Don't think there'll be much shootin' today – if it keeps on rainin', the deer will stay shelterin' in the bush. If it clears later they might come out for a feed and a warm-up in the sun.'

He opened the door with some difficulty: the storm had apparently altered the shape of the hut in some way and the door now scraped on the floor. He stepped outside and called, 'Hey, young Chris, come and 'ave a look at this!'

'Look at what, Ernie?'

'The river, mate. The bloody river, that's what.'

'Gosh. It's spread nearly right across the valley.'

'Yeah, must 'ave rained 'ard, after all. Just as well them Hobsons didn't 'ave their cattle out there.'

'What about that one?' said Chris. 'See Ernie, out in the middle of the river. Looks like it's trying to reach the shore.'

'Yeah, must 'ave been cut off last night. One they missed in the muster, I guess.'

The two men continued to watch the Hereford valiantly trying to swim to the safety of the shore. As it got carried downstream in the raging flood, its struggles were gradually carrying it into calmer water away from the main stream. It was swept out of the men's sight as the river curved round the edge of the bush.

'That one might just be lucky,' said Ernie. 'If it can keep on goin' I reckon it'll come ashore down by Hobson's house. That's if one of them big trees what's bein' swept down river doesn't collect it. At the speed some of them are travellin', a hit from one would scarper that cow.'

They continued to watch the raging torrent from the shelter of the hut doorway. Chris was amazed at the speed of the water and the size of the trees that were being carried downstream on the crest of the flood.

'Surely,' he said to himself 'the whole flat will be scoured out and ruined after this.' It did not seem possible that there would be any grazing left for the Hobson's cattle or for the deer either after the water had gone down.

'How long do you think the flood will last, Ernie?' asked Chris.

Ernie took out his battered old tobacco tin and rolled himself a cigarette, his first smoke of the day.

'All depends, mate,' he replied. 'If it stops rainin' you'll be surprised how quick it goes down. Rivers are like that 'ere. But then, if it keeps on rainin' up in the back country, the river could be in flood for a day or two. We won't get upriver today, anyway. See, the track's flooded where it crosses Katie's Creek, as yer call it. No sign of yer swimmin' pool now.'

'It appears that we'll have to stay put then,' said Chris. 'What a shame – just when we were starting to shoot some deer.'

'Take it from an old hand, boy,' said Ernie. 'If the work's not there enjoy yer day off. Yer gettin' paid for it, ain't yer? Like bein' in the army, if yer gets the chance to sit on yer arse, well, yer sit on yer arse and don't volunteer for anythin'.'

'Yes, I suppose so,' said Chris doubtfully. 'But I don't like taking money for doing nothing; it's not the way I was brought up.'

'Aw listen to him,' scoffed Ernie. 'Gettin' all goodie, good, are we, eh? Now look 'ere, boy…'

'Here's Willie,' interrupted Chris. 'Wonder what he wants.'

Willie approached along the track from the bush on his old horse, his dogs following behind. He was wearing a large oilskin coat from which his legging-clad legs protruded. On his head he wore a sou'wester hat. The dogs rushed up to Ernie and Chris and sniffed around their legs, no doubt attracted by the smell of deer. One big brute jumped up and put paws like meat plates on Ernie's shoulders, just about knocking the little guy over.

'Get in behind, yer bastards!' yelled Willie. 'G'day, youse jokers. Sorry about me dogs. Always friendly to strangers, they are. Better than takin' the arse out of yer pants, I suppose. Bit of a shower last night, eh?'

'Yeah,' agreed Ernie. 'A few spots, like. Chris 'ere, he reckoned she was pretty heavy. Now he's worried we won't be able to go shootin' today and he'll be paid to do nothin'.'

'Well he won't 'ave to worry about that now 'cos that geezer Jamieson rang through on the phone and asked me to tell yer, no more shootin'. He's comin' down today. They're goin' to put in them helicopters to shoot the deer. Somethin' to do with gettin' the meat out. Seems it's suddenly worth a few bob. Talkin' about exportin' it, they are. They reckon them Huns like the taste of it. Sounds a dag caper to me. Must be goin' to fit them helicopters up with machine-guns, like in the Korean war.'

'Hey, Willie. Does that mean we're out of a job?' asked Ernie. 'Cripes, mate, we've only just started and young Chris 'ere is shootin' real good. Better than me 'e is.'

'Don't know much more about it,' said Willie. 'Jamieson will tell yer all about it when he gets 'ere. I'd better get back. Me breakfast will be ready.'

'We saw one of yer cattle gettin' swept down the river before, Willie,' said Ernie. 'Yer musta missed it in the muster, eh? Reckon the way it was goin' it would come ashore further downstream.'

'Most likely one of them wild ones from up above the gorge. Me tally was right. If we 'ad been one short Katie would 'ave 'ad us doin' a straggle muster next day, like. Okay, see yer.'

He turned his horse round, shouted to his dogs and trotted off down the rain-sodden track towards the bush track, which was only just above water. As he disappeared into the trees, Ernie said, 'Cripes, mate, that's a bit of a bugger. I was just startin' to enjoy meself on this caper. Yer know what I mean.'

'Yes, so was I,' agreed Chris. 'You know Ernie, this has been the first time that I have experienced a feeling of genuine confidence in myself. I've got to thank you for changing my whole outlook on life.'

'Aw,' said Ernie, sounding quite embarrassed. 'Yer don't 'ave to go on like that. Yeah, yer were a bit of a know-all at first but yer admitted yer were wrong and that was a big thing to do. Now yer one of the best mates a man ever 'ad. Anyway, enough of that caper. We'll just 'ave to wait until Jamieson comes along.'

At the head of the valley the high peaks were shrugging off their blankets of cloud and rays of sunshine were sneaking through to bathe the newly fallen snow in pink and gold. The wind had changed from the north to the south west and the air had become distinctly colder. Both men were glad to don their warm jerseys and parkas. A shy sun peeped out from behind the clouds above the hut but soon withdrew, almost appearing to be reluctant to announce to the world that the storm was over.

Ernie scratched his ear and said, 'The change in the wind

should keep them sandflies away. Did yer get bitten in the night, mate? – I did.'

'No,' replied Chris. 'They don't seem to worry me much. I put on some of that Dettol and olive oil mixture of yours, too. Stinks a bit, but it seems to keep them away. A few of them must have got into the hut somehow. Did you forget about the ointment, Ernie?'

'Yeah,' he answered. 'They wouldn't 'ave much trouble gettin' in with all them cracks in the walls. Yer could drive a dozer through some of 'em.' He felt in his pockets for his tobacco tin, found it lying on the corner of the table and rolled himself a smoke. Lighting it he said, 'Looks like she might clear now. Could come out good later.'

Chris moved up wind from the pungent odour of Enrie's tobacco and said, 'Yes, it appears that way. What will you do now? It looks as though our jobs are in jeopardy.'

'If yer mean by that, we will get the boot, yeah, I reckon yer right. Should hit 'em up for a bit of compensation over it, but I don't reckon we'll get much. Them buggers are harder than a money lender's heart. A man wouldn't 'ave come away down 'ere if he'd known it was only goin' to last a few days. I would 'ave taken that farm manager's job up in North Canterbury.'

Chris, who couldn't quite imagine Ernie managing anything, let alone a farm, asked, 'Did you get a good offer, Ernie?'

'Well I saw it advertised and I could 'ave 'ad a go at it.'

'I think I might apply for a position as a helicopter shooter,' said Chris. 'Why don't you have a go at it too?'

'That'll be the day!' exclaimed Ernie. 'If yer think I'm goin' to fly round them hills and gullies in one of them things you've got another think comin'.'

'Oh, I don't know, Ernie,' said Chris brightly. 'I think it might be rather fun. I'll certainly inquire about it anyway.'

Ernie's reply was a disgusted grunt.

Down by the river a flock of seagulls squawked at each other as they gorged themselves on the grubs and worms left behind by the receding river.

'The river appears to be dropping,' said Chris.

'Yeah,' agreed Ernie. 'Now it's stopped rainin' it'll probably go down fairly quick. These 'ere Coast rivers do that. One minute yer got a flood and the next thing yer know she's all over bar the shoutin'.'

A brace of wild duck planed in to make a perfect landing on a pond and went 'bottoms up' immediately, seeking sustenance from beneath the surface of the water. From the bush behind the hut, a stag roared and was answered by another higher up the hill.

'That's two we won't get a crack at, boy,' said Ernie disgustedly. 'How the hell they're goin' to shoot 'em from helicopters in the bush, beats me. Bloody stupid I calls it. But then them desk wallers never did 'ave a clue about these things. Aw well, I'll put a brew on while we wait for Jamieson.'

CHAPTER TEN

After they had drunk their tea they sat on their bunks, Ernie filling in the time smoking and complaining about 'them stupid nitwits in Wellington what sent us down 'ere and just when we get settled and start shootin' a few of their deer, they pull the plug on the whole thing.'

Wellington, to Ernie, represented government, for which, like all forms of authority, he had the utmost contempt. Utopia to him would be a society where there was no government, police, or office wallers; the only essential thing being a never-ending supply of beer.

Just as Ernie was rolling his third cigarette, they heard the sound of an engine labouring in low gear and, going to the hut door, they saw Jamieson's Land Rover appear from the bush. It was making heavy weather of the slippery conditions on the track. It wallowed through the puddles like a duck with a gammy leg, sending up clouds of spray as it approached them. Striking a patch of firmer ground near the hut, the vehicle leapt forward only to brake in front of the door. Jamieson climbed out and greeted Chris and Ernie in his usual surly manner.

'Good day,' he said. 'Did Willie Hobson give you the message?'

'Yeah,' Ernie replied in a disgruntled tone of voice. 'He told us youse jokers are closin' down the shootin' like. What's the caper? We've only been 'ere a few days and the boy 'ere, is becomin' a crack shot. Best mate I've ever 'ad, too.'

Jamieson was surprised to hear Ernie heaping praise on Chris. When he had left them a few days before, Ernie seemed to have nothing but contempt for the youth. He shrugged his shoulders and said, 'Yeah, well, I'm not to blame for it. It's a directive we've had from Wellington. The meat is worth big money in Germany and the United States. There's talk of some cockies farming deer but I don't know how you would ever domesticate them. Anyway, they're putting the choppers in and anything they shoot will be lifted out.'

'Aw yeah,' sneered Ernie, 'and what about the ones in the bush? 'Ow yer goin' to get them, eh? Yer can't fly one of them things round in the bush. Them deer will just stay in there and laugh at yer.'

'I don't know,' replied Jamieson impatiently. 'I'm only telling you what I've been told. Now come on, pack up your gear and we'll get out of here. Oh, Chris, there's a letter for you. It was sent to the office.' He took a letter out of his pocket and passed it over, saying, 'I read in the paper how you had run all that way to get help for the people on the plane while Ernie here looked after them. That was a pretty good thing you jokers did.'

''Ow are they gettin' on in hospital?' asked Ernie.

'Good,' Jamieson answered. 'The pilot was pretty crook but he's out of danger now and he's going to be okay. His sister has already gone home. There's no doubt about it, you blokes saved their lives.'

Chris had, by this time, ripped open the envelope and extracted a sheet of expensive looking pale blue paper.

'Yes, it's from the girl,' he said. 'She wants us to call at her home next time we are in Ranginui. She says she wants to thank us personally for saving their lives.'

'Gee, mate,' laughed Ernie. 'You could be in there. Flash lookin' bint like that. There's no knowin' 'ow she might show her gratitude.'

'Oh, don't be crude.' Chris was quite embarrassed at the idea, 'I'm sure nothing would be further from her thoughts. I wonder when we'll get the chance to go there.'

'Go today if you want to,' said Jamieson. 'I've got a few things to do in Ranginui before I go home. Drop you off there and pick you up later. I presume you'll both want to come back to Port Thompson with me.'

'I'll go back with yer, mate,' said Ernie. 'Don't want to stay down 'ere now the shootin's finished. The boy 'ere reckons 'e's goin' to 'ave a go at the helicopter shootin'. Told the bugger he was mad, but he's a hell of a good shot and might be just the sort of joker yer lookin' for.'

'Is that right, Chris?' asked Jamieson 'We're hoping some of the shooters will take it on. We'll certainly give you a trial, although you have to understand that it's a lot different shooting from a moving chopper than it is from the ground.'

'Yes, I'm very interested,' replied Chris. 'And thanks for the offer to drop us off at Mary Thomas' place. It's at 85 Rimu Road.'

'I know where that is,' said Jamieson. 'We go right past it on our way in. Do you want to be dropped off too, Ernie?'

'No, let the boy go,' said Ernie. 'I'm not much good at that visitin' caper – probably go and spill me tea or somethin'. Just drop me off at a pub and I'll fill in me time there.'

By this time the two hunters had their swags packed and were all ready to leave.

'Okay, throw your gear in and we'll get going,' instructed Jamieson.

As he started the engine and moved off down the track Chris asked him where he should go to apply for a helicopter shooter's job.

'Probably best to have a yarn to Andrew Lucas,' answered Jamieson. 'His family operate Whirlybird Helicopters from the Ranginui Airport. They've got a Hughes 300 that they are fitting up for deer recovery. I'll give him a ring when we get to town, if you like. You could see the girl and then go over and have a talk to Andrew. I know the department want to get onto this as soon as possible. If Andrew's available he might come over to the Thomas place to see you.'

'Thanks,' said Chris.

The rest of the journey to town passed mostly in silence, each of the men busy with his own thoughts. Ernie wondered what he would do. Probably go back to Timber Creek. A long time since he had been there; but after all it was home, or the nearest place to home that Ernie had ever known. With a bit of luck his sister, Phyllis, and her husband would put him up for a while at the Golden Nugget. He wondered if she would even recognise him – especially with his luxuriant beard; she had probably written him off by now. Of course she would insist that he get a job, but he guessed he would be able to use his cunning to stall that one for a while. As you have no doubt already guessed, Ernie and work were not the best of mates, but occasionally a truce had to be called as he found that the dole did not quite cover his expenses. Then, very reluctantly, he was in the job market again. However, he would no doubt cross that bridge when he came to it. He wouldn't want to live at the Golden Nugget too long anyway. From what he had heard his sister was a bit jumped-up and would only fuss and insist that he wash and shower regularly and change his clothes. He wouldn't be able to smoke in their living area either, but he would dodge that part of the place whenever possible and spend most of his time in the bar where he might be able to scrounge a few drinks off his brother-in-law, Ron, who, from what he'd heard, was a pretty good bloke. With the money he would receive from the deer culling, he might be able to buy a small block of land with a bit of a hut on it. Good thought, anyway, he reckoned and, after all, old Ernie was always the ultimate optimist. Phyllis might be good for a touch too, after a while. She would probably get pretty sick of him hanging round the Golden Nugget on the bludge all the time and be willing to part with a few quid to get rid of him. Perhaps a small investment in the lottery might be worthwhile.

Jamieson slowed the Land Rover as he approached a 'Flooding' sign at the side of the road and said, 'The road was blocked to anything other than 4WD vehicles when I came up for you fellows. Apparently Mossy Creek burst its banks in last night's rain but it looks okay now.'

Indeed the road was almost clear of water. He accelerated again and they continued on towards Ranginui. The farms on both sides of the road had a wet and sodden look to them and large areas were under water. There was a cold south-west wind blowing across the flats and, even though this heralded fine weather, nobody had informed the dairy cows of that. They stood around in the saturated paddocks with their tails to the wind and their backs humped up as they grazed fitfully at the wet pasture.

'It must be hard on the animals here, when it rains like it did last night,' said Chris.

'Yeah,' agreed Jamieson. 'It is. Just imagine standing out in a paddock in that lot last night. No wonder the poor buggers look a bit dejected this morning. Still, the stock on the East Coast can get pretty stressed when there's a drought on and feed is short. No perfect place, I guess.'

They were now reaching the outskirts of Ranginui. On the left there was a big sawmill and timber treating plant. Jamieson slowed the vehicle to let a large truck and trailer unit turn in the gateway with a load of logs for the hungry saws. Almost next door, and on the same side of the road, was the factory of the Ranginui Co-op Dairy Company, which processed all the milk from the surrounding farms. About half a mile further on, a gold-dredge wrested wealth from the stony soil, its buckets and screens screaming and shrieking like the lost souls in hell.

Soon houses started to appear, most with smoke from wood fires pouring from their chimneys. The second street on the left proved to be Rimu Road and the Land Rover turned into it and stopped outside number 85, a large modern brick home set well back from the street.

'There you are, Chris,' Jamieson said as he pulled into the kerb. 'I'll pick you up later. I'll ring Andrew Lucas in a few minutes. He won't be flying today because of this wind, so he may very well come over here to see you.'

Chris climbed out and said, 'Thanks, Mr Jamieson. I'll leave my things with you if I may. Goodbye, Ernie, and thanks for all your help and friendship.'

Ernie appeared quite embarrassed. 'Aw cripes, mate, that weren't nothin'. Yer was a good cobber. Anyway, I'll see yer around. And you be careful of them helicopters.'

They shook hands and Chris turned and walked toward the wrought iron gates in the brick wall fronting the house. A gravel drive, edged with patterned river stones, curved up toward the house. Where it reached the corner of the house, the drive split in two, one section continuing on alongside the house to a double garage, the other section curving off to the right to stop at the steps leading up to an open porch and the front door. A border of pansies in full flower hugged the stones on one side of the drive and standard roses in their autumn flowering made a pleasing break between the drive and an immaculately trimmed lawn. On the other side of the drive, camellias and rhododendrons masked a paling fence. A large weeping elm, resplendent in its autumn colours, held pride of place in the centre of the lawn. In front of the garage a near-new expensive car was parked.

Chris admired the scene as he walked up the drive and climbed the steps leading to the lead-lighted front door. He rang the bell and the door was soon opened by an attractive blond haired young woman with her arm in a sling.

'Good afternoon,' he said. 'Are you Mary Thomas?

CHAPTER ELEVEN

Let us leave Chris in Ranginui and accompany Ernie back to his birthplace, Timber Creek. He did tell me some time later that Chris had taken on the helicopter shooting and he had proved to be just as successful as he had been at ground shooting. He had gained his licence to fly helicopters and was now well-known over most of the South Island as a careful and competent pilot. He had also married Mary Thomas. Ernie had received an invitation but the thought of dressing up scared him so he declined, making the excuse that he was too busy on the farm with the lambing.

Right, to get back to our friend Ernie and his departure from Ranginui and his arrival in Timber Creek. Jamieson had run him to earth at the Red Lion where he had imbibed freely and well: 'Makin' up for lost time,' he reckoned. 'Like signin' the pledge, bein' marooned away up the river with no beer.'

'Yeah,' said Jamieson. 'There's method in our madness. Supply an old soak like you with beer, Ernie, and we wouldn't get any deer shot. Right, let's get you out to the Land Rover and we'll away home.'

Jamieson and Ernie arrived at Port Thompson in the early evening. Ernie had slept most of the way up from Ranginui, his snores almost drowning out the sound of the Land Rover's diesel engine. He awoke as they were driving through the outskirts of the town and said, 'Musta dropped off, eh?'

'You sure did that all right, Ernie,' replied Jamieson. 'Sounds like it must have sobered you up too. Where do you want to be dropped off?'

'I'm goin' out to me sister's place at Timber Creek,' announced

Ernie. 'But I can't go out there at this time of the day. Wouldn't be fair to drop in on her as late as this, like. Reckon I'll 'ave to stay in town and go out in the mornin'. Might be able to cadge a ride on a loggin' truck or somethin'. Mind you, I ain't got no money to pay for a bed till youse jokers pay me.'

'Look, Ernie,' said Jamieson. 'You've had a bit of a raw deal – what with the department suddenly closing up on the shooting and putting you out of a job. I reckon they could stand you a night's accommodation at the Crown Hotel again, then I can run you out to Timber Creek in the morning. I can find a reason for going out there easy enough. I'll have your money ready then too. I'll drop you off at the Crown and pick you up at 10 am. How's that?'

That's what Ernie had wanted when he'd dropped the hint and he said, 'That's mighty good of yer, mate.'

That night Ernie rang through to his sister and told her he would be coming out next morning. 'Could yer put a bloke up for a few days, sis? Just till I get settled somewhere, like. I won't be no trouble.'

Phyllis didn't sound overenthusiastic about the idea, but supposed it would be all right as long as he behaved himself. When she mentioned it to her husband, Ron, he was quite pleased with the arrangement. Not having met Ernie, he said 'Maybe we could get him to do a few jobs around the place, like a bit of painting, gardening.'

'If Ernie is as energetic as he was when I last saw him just before he went overseas, you'll be lucky to get him out of bed in the morning, let alone do any work. He can sleep in the sleep-out at the bottom of the garden,' she said in a tone that didn't allow any argument.

CHAPTER TWELVE

I don't suppose many of you have been to Timber Creek and you must be wondering what the place is like. Well, it's halfway between being one of those places you'll miss if you blink your eyes and a mid-sized country town.

If you drive through, you'll get a feel for the place and don't worry that you'll get lost – no one's been lost in Timber Creek, no one sober that is. There was the time when old Foxy Turner got lost on his way home from the pub: his missus reported him missing to the local cop (Timber Creek had a resident constable in those days) and a search was instituted. After about a couple of hours he was found fast asleep in a shed at the back of the hall: 'Got lost,' he said.

If you head north from Port Thompson on the main drag you'll come to the town of Brannigans. There was a lot of gold came out of the creeks and rivers around Brannigans in the early days, but when the gold petered out the place sort of went to sleep. Then some guy discovered coal up in the hills behind the town and that set the place up again and now it's quite a thriving township. Through Brannigans and across the Totara River bridge, you'll see a sign to Timber Creek. It's a shingle road, but don't get your knickers in a twist over that because the council keep it pretty good. After driving through the bush for about half an hour, you'll come out onto some river flats. Once again you're on the banks of the Thompson River – good farming land, this: all river-silt country.

The first sign you'll see of Timber Creek is the sawmill about one mile from the town; that's where the tarseal starts. Incidentally, just in case you get too excited about the tarseal, I should mention that it finishes half a mile the other side of the town. The road continues on for another twenty miles where it ends at Diamond Lake. There, when the sun is shining, the lake sparkles in the sun and, surrounded by bush as it is, it looks for all the world like a diamond set in a bed of green velvet. It is a very popular place for the residents of Port Thompson to take their boats during fine summer weekends. There is a sheltered picnic area with tables, barbeques and toilets and, for those who can brave the cold water, safe swimming. Awesome trout populate the waters and, as it is a sanctuary, hundreds of duck flock to the lake in the shooting season. But beware: the sandflies can be vicious, particularly just before rain, and nothing will clear a picnic area quicker than a host of ravenous sandflies.

We had reached the sawmill. It's a typical small West Coast mill. The old sheds are built of corrugated iron that has gone rusty over the years, but the mill is run efficiently under the management of Jack Menzies and is good for employment in the district. After the mill, the road takes a gentle right-hand bend just before the township and you emerge from a small bush reserve to see Timber Creek laid out before you.

Houses typical of most country towns line both sides of the road as you go down the main street. Most have weatherboard or corrugated iron walls and iron roofs. A couple of the first ones are in a fairly dilapidated condition, their sagging verandahs bearing a sad look and almost appearing to say: 'Help me'. Their roofs are rusty and the timber walls are covered in lichen. If they were ever painted it must have been a mighty long time ago. One has three old wrecks of cars on the front lawn, or where the lawn would be if there was one. Fortunately these places are the exception rather than the rule and the other houses, in the main, are kept in good condition. Most front lawns are neatly mown and some houses have gardens, which are a blaze of colour in the summer. In the spring, camellias and rhododendrons, which thrive on the Coast, make splashes of colour for all to admire.

On the right is the former police station, now a private residence. It is a substantial brick building with a house and lock-up at the back. There used to be a resident constable in Timber Creek but five years ago the authorities, in their wisdom, closed the station and transferred the constable to Port Thompson. This almost caused a riot among some of the residents but, apart from the odd case of drunkenness or fishing without a licence, Timber Creek is a pretty law-abiding place.

The Misses Monaghan, two old maids in their seventies, live opposite in one of the neatest properties in the town. Their garden glows with colourful flowers all summer and the old dears have a cheery word for every passer-by as they toil away in their section. They have lived in the house all their lives, carrying on where their parents left off. Florrie used to run the post office and Maureen taught at the primary school. When Florrie retired, the local storekeeper, Terry Masters, took over the postal agency. It would be hard to find two more contented women – only Maureen had been off the Coast and that was when she went to training college in Christchurch.

'What would we want to go away for?' they would ask. 'We've got everything we want here: good friends, our garden, our chooks and here we can help to do the good work of the Lord through the church.'

They are devout Catholics and are proud of the fact that they live next door to the Catholic church and school, or the 'Holy City' as it is known locally. Each Saturday they can be seen taking flowers and greenery from their garden over to the church for the Sunday service. Father O'Halleron, the parish priest, lives in a small cottage adjacent to the church and another small building houses the two sisters who run the Catholic School.

By a strange quirk of fate, or maybe the sense of humour of the early settlers, the Anglican and Presbyterian churches are situated across the road. All three churches have better-than-average congregations for these days. You see, at Sunday services, there is no way the Micks are going to be outdone by the Prods and, of course, the Prods are not going to be put to shame by the Micks. Consequently, on Sunday mornings the hills resound to the sound of music as the congregations try to outsing each other. No doubt God is highly delighted with this unusual occurrence. The three men of the cloth are all good cobbers and often have a chuckle together about it.

Next to the churches a few more houses line both sides of the road, followed by a couple of empty shops – an unfortunate, but common sight in rural towns today. In a strategic position on one of the corners at the cross roads, we see the hub of the township, the Golden Nugget Hotel, and directly opposite is Laurie Scott's garage and service station with its petrol and diesel pumps on the forecourt.

Across on the other two corners are Terry Masters' general store and the two-teacher primary school. The store stocks almost everything: from the proverbial needle to the anchor.

Down the two side-streets there are more houses, some with a few acres of land. One of these houses is owned by old Paddy Hannan who, as someone once put it, is as Irish as Mick McGinty's shillelagh. He arrived in New Zealand after the First World War from County Cork and gravitated to the West Coast and Timber Creek. A great socialist (the fact that the Coast invariably elects a Labour mp appeals to Paddy's philosophy), he can always be found at political meetings, soundly berating the Tories and loud in his praise of the Labour candidate. He has lived in the old house ever since his arrival in Timber Creek and, on his retirement from the sawmill, where he doubled as saw doctor and engineer, he purchased the house and the adjoining three paddocks. Two paddocks are for his house cow and pet donkey and he keeps his collection of old machinery in the third. An inveterate hoarder of junk, Paddy can never resist a bargain and his old two ton Bedford is continually returning from forays far and near, loaded down with Paddy's 'bargains'. He calls himself a dealer but most people refer to him as collector of junk. In the five years since his retirement he has been able to concentrate on his 'business', as he calls it, and as a result the collection has grown apace.

In that paddock there is now the largest collection of old cars, trucks and tractors to be found anywhere on the Coast – and probably the South Island for that matter. There are old Dodges, Chevs, Vauxhalls and Fords; there are McCormick Deerings, Allis Chalmers and Caterpillars, all in various stages – from the complete machine to just the engine block or chassis. The grass grows around, under and through the old wrecks and around the fence lines the blackberry is poking inquisitive tendrils through windows, doors and up through floorboards. The local cockies and indeed folk from further afield are very thankful for Paddy's collection. For instance, when Angus McLean's old Caterpillar D2 expired through the left-hand drive sprocket breaking into three pieces he rang the agent. 'Yes,' they said. 'We've got one here. The cost is two hundred pounds.'

'Cripes, I only want the sprocket not the whole flamin' tractor,' he said and round to old Paddy's he went.

'Come with me, boyo' said Paddy, picking up a slasher and leading the way out to the back of his paddock. 'Sure and I've got an old D2 in here somewhere, so I have.' He slashed at some gorse and blackberry, gradually revealing an old D2 minus its tracks and motor.

'Are to be sure, Angus. That'll be what you're lookin' for,' he said, pointing to the left sprocket. 'Get that off and she's all yours, so she is.'

'How much, Paddy?' asked Angus, hardly able to believe his good fortune.

'How would a tenner suit you?' replied Paddy.

'Only ten quid, Paddy? Gee that's a gift, mate!' exclaimed Angus. He took out his tobacco and papers and rolled a smoke and passed the makings to Paddy.

'Oh to be sure, Angus, seeing as you're a Scot I'll not charge you too much. If you were an Englishman 'twould be different,' said Paddy, who, like many Irish, didn't have much time for the Poms.

So you see, Paddy and his collection are of great benefit to the community and that was the reason why the County Health Inspector got short shift from the locals when he suggested Paddy clean up his property. In his shed and on his front verandah there is a veritable Aladdin's cave of bits and pieces to make any mechanically minded man drool. Gaskets, pistons, valves, crankshafts, clutches, fan belts, engine blocks, plus nuts and bolts of all sizes hang on the walls, lie in boxes, sit on benches or are just carelessly flung on the floor. In the case of the more valued items, Paddy's house has been pressed into service, and both sides of the hall, from the front door to the kitchen, are decorated with items mechanical. The wonder of it all is that he seems to know where everything is and it only takes a few moments of fossicking to reveal the most wonderful treasures.

Paddy is quite abstemious and drinks very little. The only exception to this is on St Patrick's Day, when he dresses up in a green suit, green shirt, green tie and, with a shamrock in his buttonhole, heads for the Golden Nugget. Once there, he gives the traditional Irish greeting on entering a pub: 'God bless all here', and proceeds to consume large quantities of Irish Mist whiskey, specially procured by Ron Bassett for the occasion. Suitably fortified, he goes out on to the street and marches up and down singing 'Danny Boy' at the top of his rather good tenor voice. When the effects of the whiskey really take hold he usually collapses in a heap and is collected by the boys and taken home to bed. As you can imagine, severe the hangover is, as is the remorse, and Paddy, vowing and declaring that this is the last time, doesn't touch another drop of Irish Mist until next St Patrick's Day when the whole episode is repeated once more.

Next door to Paddy lives another character, Tubby Bourke. Nobody knows Tubby's real Christian name. Ever since he arrived in Timber Creek he has been known as Tubby. As you've probably worked out he's what is best described as rotund. Tubby can be said to 'have religion', as it used to be known. He will come into the Golden Nugget with a sad look on his craggy old face and say that he's been having a yarn to God on the phone and God reckoned things weren't going too well. One day he said that God must be annoyed with him because He wasn't answering His phone, but then a few days later he'd got through to God and everything was okay again, and he looked as happy as a kid with two ice creams. When we asked him what God thought of him drinking beer, he said that God had never said he couldn't, so he guessed it must be all right. We reckoned that he had never asked. Everyone tolerates him and nobody makes fun of him.

Further down the main road we come to the community centre and the sports ground with its war memorial gates. In the winter rugby is played here on Saturdays in the winter and Rugby League on Sundays, some young fellows turning out for both to make up the numbers.

Over the road from the community centre and next to the school is the council yard and the grader driver's house. Rangi Tainui not only drives the grader but the council tip-truck as well. A couple of years ago the council, at Rangi's request, employed Ernie to drive the truck for a few days, but after getting the truck bogged down twice, (the second time a bulldozer had to be brought up from Port Thompson to extricate it) and tipping three loads of shingle in the wrong place, the council decided that they could do without his services and, if necessary, employ the local cartage contractor, whose yard is next door.

Amongst the last few houses on the main street is the only two storey house in Timber Creek. Bridie O'Gorman has lived there on her own since her husband, Mick, died at the early age of fifty-two a few years ago. Some say that poor old Mick departed from this life to get away from Bridie's tongue, which is as sharp as a cut-throat razor. Maybe this is a bit cruel but Mick did spend most of the little bit of free time she allowed him either fishing in the river or hunting for deer in the hills. Others say that he was only permitted to go hunting was because Bridie was always looking for a bit of free meat. I don't know whether she actually physically abused Mick but he frequently appeared at work with a black eye, a split lip or a bloody nose. When asked about it he always said that he had run into a door – perhaps he should have removed all the doors and hung up curtains. You know, you can talk all you like about battered wives but we reckoned that Mick was a classic example of a battered husband. She is known in Timber Creek as The Widow Woman and is avoided by most people because of her caustic tongue. Even Father O'Halloran is scared of her and has been known to duck out of sight when she approaches.

Pass a disused blackberry-enshrouded blacksmith shop on the left and you're out of town.

CHAPTER THIRTEEN

As I said earlier, Ernie's sister, Phyllis, was not pleased at the idea of Ernie coming to stay. When she saw him get out of Jamieson's Land Rover, she was even more displeased. He was shorter than she remembered, but what really put her off the idea of sharing her house with him were his filthy clothes and his big bushy beard. Never had she seen a beard like it and she made a resolution there and then to get that monstrous hairy mass removed at the first possible opportunity.

Ernie grabbed his swag off the back of the vehicle and came trotting over to Phyllis.

'G'day, Sis,' he greeted. 'Nice to see yer again. Been a long time, eh?'

'Yes,' replied Phyllis uncertainly. 'Please don't call me Sis. My name is Phyllis. When are you going to get that horrible beard shaved off? It's not going to look at all nice at the Golden Nugget.'

'Aw, I don't know,' said Ernie. 'You remember when we was young and you had all them children's Bibles and that? All the pictures in 'em showed that most of God's mates had beards. Yer should be pleased, S…er Phyllis.'

'Yes, well that's beside the point,' said Phyllis, deciding to leave that matter alone for the time being. 'You had better come inside and remove those filthy clothes and have a shower. Have you got any clean clothes?'

'No,' Ernie confessed. 'Yer see there weren't no way of washin' up in the bush.'

'Oh well, I'll find something of Ronald's for you to wear while I wash yours. How a brother of mine could get in such a state I don't know. Whatever would Mother have thought?'

After a shower and a change into clean clothes, which were far too big for him, Ernie was much more presentable to his sister. 'If only he would get rid of that beard,' she thought. 'Oh well, I suppose blood is thicker than water; although sometimes you do wonder.'

Ernie spent about two months living at the Golden Nugget with his sister and brother-in-law. During this time he made the acquaintance of the regulars at the pub; some of us, me included, had never met him before but we soon got to know him, especially his capacity for beer. Others like Ces Draper had known him back in their school days before the war.

It was easy to see that Phyllis resented him being there; even though he occupied the sleep-out down the back of the garden and kept out of her way as much as possible. Many were the arguments that she and Ron had over Ernie. Ron thought him quite a good old bloke, always ready for a laugh, although you did have to watch that he took his turn to shout. He helped out a bit around the place; serving behind the bar when it was busy on a Saturday, and once he even did a bit of gardening, until Phyllis caught him pulling out freshly planted marigold plants, mistaking them for weeds. After that episode, gardening was out as far as Ernie was concerned.

One day, about one o'clock, a Port Thompson land agent called in for a drink and in the course of conversation, told us that the Trotter Block up Pegleg Creek was for sale. He reckoned it was going cheap on account of its run down state. Two hundred acres, a one room hut, a hundred Romneys and a dog thrown in for good measure.

'How much?' asked Ernie.

'What would you do with a farm, Ernie?' questioned Ron.

'I'd like to 'ave a block of land,' replied Ernie as he pulled himself another beer. 'Bloke's always been keen on ownin' a bit of New Zealand. Besides, it would get me away from me sister. Fair gettin' on me goat she is, always naggin' on about me beard and me clothes and that. Reckon she'd be glad to see the back of me.'

'Yeah,' agreed Ron. 'You might be right, mate. She's been bloody hard to live with since you came to live with us. No offence, like.'

'How the hell could you afford a farm, Ernie?' asked someone. 'Yer reckon yer can't afford to crack yer whip half the time.'

'Got a bit of money, mate,' boasted Ernie. 'Yeah, remember? I won a bit on the lottery a coupla weeks ago, and I've got me cheque for the deer cullin'. I could get a mortgage and I bet me sister would put up a bit just to see the back of me.' He turned to the agent and said, "Ow much for the place, mate?'

'Well,' answered the agent, who could see a possible sale and was anxious to off-load what he considered was a liability to his business. 'They're asking 2000 bucks for it but I reckon you could get it for 1800. What say you put in an offer?'

Ernie, who had been doing a bit of arithmetic on the back of an old envelope, said, 'Tell yer what I'll do with yer. If I can get a mortgage from the bank and Sis will give me a couple of hundred quid, you've got a deal.'

'It's 400 dollars now, Ernie. We've gone decimal don't forget. Anyway, you haven't got a show of getting four hundred dollars out of Phyllis,' sneered Ron. 'With what she was saying about you last night after you had spilt that beetroot on her new white tablecloth I don't reckon she would give you the time of day.'

'What do yer bet?' said Ernie. 'Tell yer what, if I can get the money out of her you wipe me slate clean in the bar.'

'Okay,' laughed Ron, thinking he was quite safe. 'It's a deal.'

'Don't you want to see the place?' asked the agent, thinking that all this sounded promising, provided that old Ernie could twist his sister's arm.

'Nar,' said Ernie. 'Been up there when I was a kid. Just the place for me. No road access. Keep parasites like salesmen, land agents and Jehovah's Witnesses away.'

The agent opened up his case and took out an 'Offer to Purchase' form which he filled in for 1800 dollars subject to finance.

'Okay Ernie,' he said. 'Just sign here and initial here and here and we'll see how we go.'

Most of us were amazed at Ernie being so keen on owning a block of land and hoped he knew what he was about. What we didn't know at that stage was that he had, as a kid, found traces of gold in Pegleg Creek and some of its tributaries. Shrewd old bugger, Ernie.

He said to the agent that he would go and change his clothes and get a ride into town to see the bank manager. When he came back about half an hour later it was with a big grin on his face. Well, we supposed he had a grin on his face: the beard didn't permit us to see his mouth but the twinkle in his eyes and the chuckles that he gave made us think that he was grinning.

'Better wipe the slate clean, Ron,' he said. 'Sis has given me a couple of hundred bucks. Told yer she would. Reckoned it was worth it to see the back of me.'

He looked a bit more presentable in a clean shirt and trousers. He had also had a lick and a spit wash, which he was sure would impress the bank manager.

Ernie got the agent to drop him off at the bank in town. The manager didn't look very enthusiastic when Ernie was shown into his office, but Ernie *was* a returned serviceman and the bank had instructed all its managers to give special consideration to those who had been away and fought for their country. Also, the bank was as keen as the land agent to see the Trotter Block sold. The present owners owed a lot of money on it and were behind with their interest payments. Of course, as is the way with all bankers, he didn't show too much enthusiasm. I reckon that as part of their training, bankers are taught to be as negative as possible. If it's a woman's prerogative to have a headache it must be a banker's to say 'no'. Not much fun in a banker's household!

However, our Ernie is renowned for his glib tongue and his

tenacity, and in short time he had extracted an undertaking from the bank to make up the difference between his lottery winnings and his deer-culling cheque, together with his sister's contribution, and the purchase price.

'Are you sure your sister will help, Mr O'Neil?' the manager asked.

'Sure will,' replied Ernie. 'Wants me out of the place. Reckons I lower the tone of the Golden Nuggett. Be glad to see the back of me. She doesn't like me beard, see?'

'Well, I can appreciate that,' said the manager, thinking that, in granting Ernie a loan, he would be doing Mr and Mrs Bassett a good turn. They were very respected clients of the bank. 'Okay, get your sister to ring me confirming this and draw your army gratuity. Then come back and see me and we'll arrange your loan.'

'Good oh, mate!' said Ernie. 'Pleasure to do business with yer. Of course I'll want a bit extra to buy a bit of transport, like. Got me eye on an old Model A Ford ute that a cobber's got for sale. Only wants a couple hundred bucks for it.'

'Look, get this other business fixed up first and then we'll see about that. Musn't get too heavily committed, must we? Good day to you, Mr O'Neil.'

The manager got up and held the door open for Ernie to leave. As he shut the door he offered up a short prayer to the patron saint of bankers, hoping that he had done the right thing.

In a matter of about three weeks Ernie owned a farm. Well, a so-called farm. Of course the boys at the pub started to refer to him as a bloated capitalist, the landed gentry, etc.

'Be votin' for the Tories now, I suppose,' said Rangi. 'All the cockies vote for them jokers, eh?'

'And what's wrong with voting for the Tories?' asked Ron. This, of course, started an argument on the merits of the National and Labour Parties, and argumentative throats become dry throats, which require frequent lubrication. This, of course, suited Ron fine as he sold more beer. Ernie moved up into the one-room hut on his property and immediately christened it 'The Mansion'.

'See,' said one of the boys. 'Told yer he would be gettin' all uppity once he became a squatter.'

Phyllis felt some celebration was called for and suggested that she and Ron have a sherry before dinner. One sherry turned into a few sherries and, as Phyllis seldom drank, the effect was rather severe and Ron had to put her to bed. Next morning, suffering a splitting headache, she immediately blamed Ernie for her condition. Ron tried to point out that really Ernie had nothing to do with it as he wasn't even there, but Phyllis was adamant and wondered why the good Lord had seen fit to saddle her with a brother like Ernie.

Fortunately there was enough rough furniture in the hut to satisfy Ernie's frugal needs and some of the boys had gone through their sheds and found they had a surplus hammer, saw or wire strainer. The Misses Monaghan, kind old souls that they are, gave Ernie enough jam, bottled fruit and pickles to last him a long time and Laurie Scott's wife saw him off with a fruit cake and a big batch of scones. The boys wanted to have a celebration party at the pub but Phyllis told Ron that, if he allowed that lot to have a party in her pub, she was leaving; so Ron made arrangements for it to be held up at the mill, which was well away from the town.

CHAPTER FOURTEEN

One day some of the boys decided to take a trip up Pegleg Creek to see if Ernie was at home. We thought that he should have settled in, as he'd been there about three months and, when he was in the Golden Nugget the previous Saturday, he reckoned she was pretty good up there. Nice and quiet, like.

We took the Thompson River Flats Road for about five miles until we came to Jock McKenzie's road gate. The track into Ernie's place starts at Jock's yard. Jock and his wife, Fiona, had been on their place for about twenty years. When they took over it was one of the most run-down farms in the district. A lot of it was still in bush or had only been cut over and never stumped. Jock had milled the standing timber and with the proceeds had started to develop the farm. Twenty years later the whole area was in lush ryegrass and white clover pastures. Fences were neat and stockproof. The buildings were spick and span under a coat of fresh paint and pure-bred Friesian dairy cows grazed the lush pastures and produced plenty of milk for Jock's towns supply quota. Fiona was a keen gardener and brilliant flowers of all colours greeted visitors at her door.

There is a story that a few years ago Jock was escorting the Presbyterian parson round the farm. The parson, a country bloke, was interested in Jock's development and remarked that it was marvellous what God and man could achieve when they worked together. 'Yeah,' said Jock, 'but then you should have seen what it was like when God had it on his own.'

There was no road access into Ernie's place, only a track suitable for a tractor, so we left the car in Jock's yard and walked up the gorge. Ernie's old Model A ute was parked in the yard so he had to be home. Jock decided to come with us so, shouldering our packs containing the beer and some food, we set off.

Steep cliffs lined both sides of the gorge and Pegleg Creek twisted and wound its way down through the narrow flats between the cliffs. A few stunted trees were growing on the creek banks, festooned with debris and flotsam from the floods which sometimes swept down the gorge. Rocks, some as big as a small car, had been deposited in the creek bed as though flung there by a giant hand.

After about half an hour's walk, during which time we crossed the creek on three occasions, the fastidious among us removing their socks and boots, we arrived at a rusty old barbed wire fence stretching from one side of the gorge to the other. Most of the posts had broken off so the fence was, in the main, lying on the ground and of little use. Between two large moss covered strainer posts there was a Taranaki gate, kept closed even though any old Romney worth her salt could walk over the fence on either side. I opened the gate, being careful not to rip my trousers on the barbed wire, so that everyone could file through.

From here on the track followed the left-hand side of the flat for a short distance. It then deserted the creek and bent round to disappear into one of the many patches of manuka scrub with which Ernie's property was infested. The flats then widened out into quite an extensive area, all good river-silt land and well worthy of development – not that our friend Ernie was likely to be too interested in that. A couple of pukekos, their tails flicking, searched for food among the long rank grass.

'That was the last creek crossing, boys,' announced Jock.

'Does that mean we don't have to take our boots and socks off again?' asked Ces.

'Yeah,' replied Jock. 'I don't know why you bothered. Your feet would have soon dried out and they probably wanted washing anyway. Only a wee way now and we're there.'

Soon afterwards we came upon Ernie's residence. The old hut

stood close by three big beech trees. A sad and sorry old netting fence surrounded the building and from a sagging wooden gate a shingle path led up to a verandah. A large river boulder served as a doorstep.

Close by the hut there was a tumbledown old shed. The unpainted wooden walls appeared to be held up by the lichen growing on them and the rusty corrugated iron roof was almost completely hidden beneath the tendrils of a giant blackberry bush growing nearby. A workbench, covered in an assortment of tools, some so old and rusty as to be almost unrecognisable, ran across the back wall of the shed. Above the bench was the shed's only window, devoid of glass and nearly obscured by spiders' webs and blackberry vines. A bundle of opossum traps hung from the roof and a couple of sheepskins were draped across a wire strung across the shed. One corner was occupied by a part-bale of wool and next to that were a few bales of mouldy looking hay. Three black Orpington chooks pecked away in the dirt on the floor. Another one emerged from the hay bales, announcing triumphantly to the world that she had laid an egg. Three coils of barbed wire and a few old sacks just about completed the contents of the shed. Nearby the butts of a heap of silver pine posts protruded from another large patch of blackberry.

'One thing,' remarked Rangi, 'Old Ernie'll never go short of a feed of blackberries, eh?'

'No,' agreed Jock. 'Got a few hen eggs too, by the look of it. Reminds me of my place when me and Fiona first moved in.'

'Yeah,' said Ces. 'But I bet Ernie doesn't make the place as neat as yours, Jock.' This was something we all agreed about.

As we left the shed and headed across the yard to the hut, two big rats, chased by Ces' fox terrier, who had suddenly arrived on the scene, ran out of the shed and into the blackberry.

'Bloody dog,' growled Ces. 'Thought he was tied up at your place, Jock.'

'Looks like he slipped his collar,' said Jock.

We filed through the gate and walked up the path to the verandah. A long bench, made out of a slab of twelve-by-one and supported by empty kerosene boxes, ran off to the right of the door, on it there was an enamel basin half full of dirty water and beside it a cake of Lifebuoy soap. A dirty looking old towel was draped over the edge of the bench. A gold pan, a shovel with a broken handle, a honey tin of staples, a hammer and a collection of other junk took up the rest of the bench.

To the left of the door a rickety looking chair held pride of place and had a shovel and pick leaning against it. Overhead a piece of number eight wire served as a clothes-line and draped over it were a pair of jeans and a flannelette shirt. On the wall hung a galvanised hip bath. At the end of the verandah there was a stack of beer crates full of empty bottles. Rangi knocked at the door and a dog barked inside. The door opened and there stood Ernie in his singlet and long woollen underwear.

'G' day, youse jokers,' greeted Ernie. 'Yer should o' let me know yer was comin'. I could 'ave cleaned up a bit, like. But anyway come into me mansion. Just watch out for that rotten board by the door. Goin' to fix it one of these days when I get time, like. That's the bloody trouble, findin' time to do all the jobs that want doin' when yer first take over a property'.

There was only one way to describe Ernie's hut: rough with a capital 'R'. The undulating floor had a couple of ragged old chaff sacks for mats. There was a wood stove with a tin chimney on one wall. On the rough mantelpiece above the stove there was a conglomeration of junk. Strangely enough, in the middle of the mantelpiece sat a very fine chiming clock, a legacy from his mother – that it didn't work worried him not: 'Who wants to know the time?' he asked. There was an empty bottle with a candle in it, a pile of letters, mostly unpaid bills, jammed in behind a West Coast schooner. At one end was a stack of paperbacks for, surprisingly enough, Ernie had become quite a keen reader; a legacy, no doubt, from his deer culling days when he borrowed the Western novel from Chris. A big table took up most of the space in the middle of the room. On it there was a stack of old *Weekly News*, left there by the previous owners, together with cracked plates and cups and a box of old cutlery. A half loaf of bread and a part pack of butter rubbed shoulders with a box of shotgun cartridges and a skinning knife in a leather sheath. Above the mantelpiece, on hooks fastened in the wall, hung an old ex army .303, a .22 and a shotgun. Jutting out from the wall opposite the stove was Ernie's bunk, unmade of course. Some old clothes hung on nails on the walls and a kerosene lamp with a smoky chimney hung from the ceiling. The old dog, which barked when we arrived, had curled up on the chaff sack in front of the stove, his nose twitching as he dreamed of succulent joints of juicy mutton.

'What's the old mutt's name?' asked Rangi.

'Rather,' replied Ernie.

'Rather!' exclaimed Ces. 'What sort of name is that for a dog?'

'Well, yer see,' explained Ernie as he bent down and patted the tyke's head. 'He'd rather be sleepin' there than workin'.'

So, now you've heard about Pegleg Creek, you should be able to find your way up there on your own next time. Might be a good idea to let Ernie know you're coming, though, and then he won't have to meet you in his underwear – it's a pretty terrible sight, especially if you've got women or kids with you.

CHAPTER FIFTEEN

As previously mentioned, Ernie knew that there was gold in Pegleg Creek from his forays up there as a kid. Soon after his arrival, he borrowed a gold pan from old Mick McGuire. The fact that he hadn't returned the pan didn't seem to worry him and, when Mick was thrown off his horse and killed one dark night on his way home from the pub, Ernie decided he might as well keep it – Mick was unlikely to need it where he was going. He registered a gold claim at the office in Port Thompson and the money he got from the gold helped to eke out his dole. His beer money he called it. The 100 ewes (more or less) which fossicked for grass among the gorse, stumps and manuka that infested the rich alluvial soil, produced a few lambs each year. Some of these made up the bulk of Ernie's diet, supplemented by the odd deer or rabbit which fell to his rifle. He purchased potatoes, bread, tea and other necessities at the store in Timber Creek when he went in each week-end.

Every week or two he took a lamb carcass into his brother-in-law at the Golden Nugget. Of course Phyllis didn't know that the meat came from Ernie's flock. There is no way she would have accepted a lamb that had been slaughtered and dressed by her brother. Strangely enough, Ernie was a very neat butcher – probably the result of his having worked at the freezing works in Canterbury. Anyway, Ron managed to keep the source of their meat from her. It also stopped her complaining about her brother not paying his bar account because that is what the meat did. It was a completely cashless transaction, of which, the Social Security Department naturally knew nothing either. Ernie had no conscience about putting one over the government. 'Pack of sharks,' he said. 'Always bleedin' a man dry, wantin' him to pay taxes and that.' The idea of him paying taxes was about as likely as the West Coast winning the Ranfurly Shield.

Eventually, after being up the gorge for about six months, Ernie decided that he needed some form of transport for his meagre supplies, so he went to a clearing sale down south and bought an old horse, which he was assured was a docile animal and an excellent packhorse. The old nag looked docile, all right. In fact, it was so docile as to be bone lazy. Ernie rode it home, taking three days over the journey. I'm not sure whether it was the horse or Ernie that required the frequent rests but, by a strange coincidence, these rests always seemed destined to take place at one of the many pubs along the main road.

A few days after arriving home, Ernie decided to put the pack saddle, (which he had found in the back of the shed) on the horse and go down to Jock's and then on into Timber Creek in the old Model A. He dragged the saddle out from the rubbish in the back corner and, after mending a couple of straps with baling wire and binder twine, lugged it over to where the horse was tied up to the fence beside the gate. The horse, with more vigour than anyone would have thought possible, showed the white of its eyes, snorted, and pulled back on the rotten rope. The rope snapped and the old nag took off for the scrub like the winner of the Melbourne Cup.

'Hey, come back, yer mangy bastard!' yelled Ernie as he galloped off after the horse, his little bandy legs pumping away like the pistons in a V8 motor. His old dog, Rather, loped along behind. After about half an hour of scrub bashing, he came upon the horse cropping grass in a clearing down near the creek.

'Nice horse,' said Ernie in a soothing tone of voice as he sneaked up closer to the animal. The horse raised its head, gave a snort, trotted on a few paces and then stopped again and resumed feeding. Ernie swore and looked at his dog.

'Don't you bark either, yer miserable cur. If yer do I'll take it that yer laughin' at me and then I'll 'ave yer bloody guts for garters.'

The old dog wagged his tail and then lay down to swat flies and enjoy the fun.

Ernie advanced on the horse again and this time the old prad stayed still. The truth of it was, he was about as buggered as Ernie. A truce was called and Ernie got hold of the rope and started to lead the horse home. As soon as they came within sight of the pack saddle, the old nag got a new lease of life and started to play up again but this time Ernie was ready for him.

'Hold up there, yer mongrel,' he said. 'I'm not goin' to put that pack saddle on yer. From now on the only saddle you'll 'ave on will be the ridin' saddle.'

The amazing thing is that the horse seemed to understand what Ernie was saying and he quietened down immediately; he shook his head, blew through his nostrils, and nuzzled Ernie's arm with his nose.

'Go on with yer, yer old sod,' said Ernie. 'Tryin' to kid a joker now, are yer? All right then, yer can stay on the place.' He removed the rope and, giving the horse a slap on the rump, sent him away off up the creek.

'Bloke must be gettin' soft in his old age,' he murmured. 'And you can wipe that bloody sneer off yer mug too, yer useless dog, and tell me what I'm goin' to do now for transport.'

He walked back to the hut and took out a bottle of beer from the crate that he had, with great difficulty, managed to carry on his back from Jock's place. He knocked the top off on the verandah rail, sat down in his rickety old chair, and took a long swig from the bottle.

'Ah,' he said. 'That's better. Nothin' like chasin' a horse to give a man a thirst. What we want, dog, is a wee Fergie tractor like Jock's to go up and down the gorge. Tomorrow I'll 'ave another go at the gold.'

Next morning, after his usual breakfast of bacon and eggs,

he collected up his shovel and gold pan and set off up the creek with the dog. When they reached the junction with Matchbox Creek, Ernie turned off and went upstream. 'Never tried Matchbox before, Rather,' he said. 'Just might be a bit of colour up 'ere. It don't look like nobody's ever 'ad a go at it.'

The old horse was grazing away at the junction and Ernie said to him, 'G'day, yer old flea bag. Made yerself at 'ome, ain't yer?'

A short distance upstream he found a likely spot and started to pan for gold. The first dishful yielded some good colour and, the more he washed, the better it became. By eleven o'clock he had quite a bit of gold in his jar – including three good-sized nuggets. The gleam in his eye just about matched the gleam of the gold in his jar.

'Enough for today, dog,' he said. 'Don't want to over do it, do we?'

He headed off home, determined to be back the next day.

Next morning after breakfast, Ernie and his dog were away off up Matchbox Creek again. Ernie had another good day and the dog enjoyed it too, as it put the boss in a good mood and assured him of a particularly juicy bone that night. Ernie's luck held out all week and then, as often happens, the gold ran out.

'Aw well, mate,' he said to the dog. 'We've got enough there for a while. We'll go into town tomorrow and see what she's worth. Be more up there I reckon, if a guy searches for it.'

Next morning he caught the horse, saddled him up and rode off down the gorge to Jock's place, the dog following behind. He coaxed his old Model A into action and set off for town, his dog riding on the back and barking all the way.

Earnie's ute was a legend unto itself by this time and most folk recognised it as it went clattering up and down the road. It had originally been a tourer but during the war one of its many previous owners had converted it into a half ton truck. This had enabled that particular owner to acquire a special petrol ration for a commercial vehicle. When Ernie bought the old heap it was obviously feeling the effects of a hard life, plus a diet of power kerosene to help eke out the petrol ration. Ownership by Ernie didn't exactly improve the condition of something which was already clapped out. Rust, commonly known as West Coast borer, was starting to devour various parts of the old bus and Ernie's driving ability, or lack of it, plus his inattention to such things as oil changes and greasing, were all having their affect. The front bumper was tied on with baling wire and only one headlamp worked. What was left of the muffler hung on with number 8 wire and a sheet of corrugated iron covered the various holes in the deck. The two front tyres were about as bald as Ernie but, as the crate's top speed was about twenty-five miles per hour, there was little likelihood of a serious accident from a blowout. The spare was his best tyre and he had a couple of new retreads in Jock's shed, but he wouldn't put them on the ute because, as he said, 'I'm makin' sure I get me money's worth out of them old ones.' It was quite common to see Ernie driving along and for the motor to suddenly develop the most alarming rattles and clatters. He would pull up, get out, and proceed to top up the engine from a two gallon can of waste oil off the back. Most of the rattles would cease and he would climb back in and proceed on his merry way.

CHAPTER SIXTEEN

Once in town, he drove straight to the local gold buyers and parked outside. He switched off the wheezy old engine and the dog stopped barking and lay down on the deck and went to sleep.

'There yer are, yer mutt,' said Ernie to the dog. 'You're in charge.'

He crossed the footpath and went into the gold buyer's office. The office, due to its plush look, always held Ernie in some awe. However, our Ernie was pretty brazen and he marched up to the counter and said, 'G'day. I've got a bit of gold 'ere you'd better 'ave a shufti at, eh?'

'Ha!' exclaimed the gold buyer, 'struck it rich, have you?'

'Yeah, not a bad lot', said Ernie as he passed over his haul.

''Struth. You have struck it rich. Let me weigh that out,' the buyer took the gold over to his scales and continued, 'You know, you're a lucky old blighter, Ernie, the price of gold went up fifteen quid an ounce overnight.' He took up his calculator and did his sums. 'Okay, Ernie. I can give you a cheque for three thousand dollars for that lot.'

'Cripes!' exclaimed Ernie, hardly able to believe his ears. 'That's more money than I've ever 'ad. I'll be able to go and buy me wee Fergie now. See yer, mate.'

He hurried out and went into the bank, almost next door. The manager, who was out of his office talking to one of his tellers, looked up as the door opened. 'Oh hell,' he said. 'There's that little bastard, O'Neil again. He needn't think he can get any money out of this bank. He's lazy, unreliable and he's got no security.'

Ernie spied the manager and called out brightly, "Ow yer goin', Mr Francis? I've got some business to transact.'

'Not here, you haven't,' said the manager. 'The answer to whatever you want is 'no'.'

'Yeah, bloody typical. 'No' is about the only word you parasites know. Well this time it's different. I've got a cheque 'ere for three thousand bucks and I want to open an account.' He waved the cheque at the manager who, at the sight of money, got a cunning gleam in his eyes, as bankers are wont to do. However, he was not going to make it easy for the little man.

'You had an account with the bank, my friend,' he said. 'And you let us down on it. That money will have to go towards what you owe us.'

'That'll be the day,' replied Ernie. 'Yer wrote it all off. I can always go elsewhere and then I'd 'ave to tell 'em 'ow yer turned me down.'

This was the last thing Mr Francis wanted. After all, he was in enough trouble already and he didn't want his rivals to hear how he had refused money from a client – and a returned serviceman at that. He remembered how Ernie had come in and got a mortgage and 'working capital' from the bank when he bought the Trotter Block. Ernie was supposed to pay his interest and principal each month, but Ernie had seen fit to ignore both these payments and letters from the bank. In the end, Head Office had decided that the loan should be written off and had chastised the manager for making the advance in the first place. It was only because the bank did not want the Trotter Block back on its hands that it had decided to take this line. Also, Ernie found out that, for some obscure reason, the bank had failed to take security over the property, and he was therefore able to thumb his nose at them. He could talk his way out of an opossum trap, could Ernie, his mates reckoned.

'All right, Mr O'Neil. We'll give you one more chance. Jane please take care of Mr O'Neil and his cheque, will you?' With that the manager turned on his heel and took refuge in his office. Somehow he had that feeling that this would not be his day.

The cheque lodged, Ernie left the bank, the proud possessor of a cheque book. The young lady had tried to tell him of his obligations now that he had an account with the bank, but Ernie had remonstrated with her and said, 'Now you show some respect for your client or I'll be forced to contact your Wellington office.'

She was quite taken aback as she had never heard old Ernie speak like this before. 'Old beggar must have been taking elocution lessons,' she said to herself.

Ernie hurried back to his ute which, wonder of wonders, fired up straight away.

'Bloody good sign, that,' he reckoned, 'when the old bus starts first pop. Reckon it's me lucky day. Now round to West Coast Tractors to see what they've got.' With the dog barking on the back, he shot out from the kerb, narrowly missing a passing car. The driver shook his fist at Ernie and blew his horn. Ernie gave him the two fingers and shouted, 'Up yours too, mate.'

It was only a short distance round to the garage and he accomplished it without further incident; another good sign. He pulled up in the yard and switched off with the usual loud backfire and silence from the dog. This brought forth a worried-looking salesman from the office, 'Oh it's only you, Ernie,' he said with a sigh of relief. 'I thought some bugger was trying to blow the place up. What can we do for you? Might as well tell yer now, we can't trade the old ute.'

'Don't want to trade the ute, mate,' said Ernie. 'I've come in to 'ave a look at them used tractors. Thinkin' of somethin' like a wee Fergie.'

The salesman laughed and said, 'Don't tell me yer thinking of developing the farm.' He remembered a trip up the gorge to see Ernie a few months previously, when he had heard that Ernie had been boasting in the pub about how he was going to break in the farm. The salesman, not knowing Ernie and being new to the job, had shot off up to the farm, determined to beat the opposition to the sale of a tractor and implements for the development. After walking over the rough track in his light shoes and getting his feet thoroughly wet crossing the creek, he found out that Ernie had no money or intentions of breaking in the farm. A few days later he met the State Advances man, who had been conned into making the trip up the creek. He was able to speak more bluntly than the salesman and told Ernie that there was no way that the government would waste money on such a hopeless proposition. He was ordered off the property with the remark, 'If them parasites in Wellington don't want the extra production they can go and get knotted.'

'Look, matey,' said Ernie to the salesman, 'All I want is an old tractor and trailer to get me things up the gorge from Jock McKenzie's place. Of course, yer never know, a man might do a bit of development as time and money permit, like. Anyway, what 'ave youse jokers got?'

'Got a good Fordson Major going cheap at sixteen,' said the salesman. 'That's the cash price, of course.' He knew that the cash angle would stymie Ernie.

'Nah,' said Ernie scornfully. 'I don't want one of them gas-guzzling monsters. Jock McKenzie had one and he reckoned he couldn't keep the petrol up to it and it couldn't pull a hen off its nest.'

'Aw, go on,' scoffed the salesman who had been trying to off-load the old Fordson for some time.

'It's right,' assured Ernie. 'Hey! look at that. There's the tractor for me.' He hurried over to a little grey Ferguson that was parked by the fence. Right next to it was a two ton trailer. 'Gee mate, if that's not the bee's knees,' Ernie climbed up onto the seat and, grinning at the salesman, asked, 'How much?'

The salesman, having met Ernie before, wasn't all that interested. 'Two thousand cash,' he said, wishing that Ernie would get into his ute and beat it. The dog had been sniffing round the salesman's flash Cortina and, finding a wheel that looked like it needed washing, Rather lifted his leg.

'Ha, ha, the dog likes yer car,' laughed Ernie. 'He only does that on cars that 'e likes.'

'Bloody mongrel,' yelled the salesman. He picked up a stone and threw it at the dog, accidentally hitting the rear door panel of the car. 'Now look what you've made me do. Dented my car. Look Ernie, are you going to buy a tractor or not? Because, if you're only here to waste my time, I suggest you get in your old heap and bugger off.'

'No need to take that attitude,' said Ernie. 'Haven't I told yer I want this 'ere wee beauty. Tell yer what I'll do; I'll give yer eighteen hundred bucks cash and yer throw in the trailer.'

'Did you say cash?'

'Yeah, I've got me cheque-book 'ere,' boasted Ernie, waving his new cheque-book in the salesman's face.

The salesman, anxious to get rid of Ernie and his dog said, 'Okay, but you don't take possession until the bank clears the cheque. You'd better come into the office and we'll do the paperwork. Look, for God's sake, lock that bloody mongrel up in your ute – he's christened the other three wheels on my car.'

'Get in the truck, yer useless mutt,' yelled Ernie. 'Can't lock 'im in, mate. Me locks don't work and anyway, he'd just jump out the window. Can't wind them up either.'

At one word from Ernie, the dog usually did as he liked, but this time he must have thought discretion was the better part of valour and he clambered in and lay down on the seat. 'Bugger's gettin' cheeky,' said Ernie. 'Usually 'e rides on the back.'

They trooped into the office and the salesman went round behind his desk and sat down. 'Take a pew, Ernie,' he said, waving Ernie to a chair. He slid open a drawer in his desk and took out an invoice book. 'Right, you give me a cheque for eighteen hundred bucks and she's yours, that's as long as your cheque doesn't bounce, of course.'

'Now cut it out, mate,' said Ernie angrily. 'I've told yer me money's good. Now you'll deliver it for that price, won't yer?'

'Cripes no,' protested the salesman. 'What do you take us for, a charitable institution or something? We're losing money on the deal as it is. You'll have to pick it up here.'

'Gee, that's a pity,' said Ernie. 'Reckon I might 'ave to go and see what the other blokes 'ave got. And I bet me dog's fair bustin' for another leak by now.'

Most salesmen and women were usually pretty anxious to see the back of Ernie and this guy was no exception.

'Yeah, okay,' he agreed. 'We'll deliver it out to Jock's farm, soon as your cheque is cleared. How will I let you know? You don't have a phone, do you?'

'No,' replied Ernie, 'got no one I want to ring up, 'ave I? Just tell Jock and he'll let me know and then I'll ring yer up and make a time.' The salesman thought that this was typical of Ernie: got no one to ring up and then, in the next sentence, says he will give a joker a ring. Oh well, you meet all sorts.

'Okay Ernie,' the salesman said with a sigh of relief, thinking that his ordeal was almost over. He stood up and reluctantly put out his hand, which Ernie grasped in his hoary old palm. When he shook hands, he really did the job properly and the salesman was sure he could hear and feel his fingers being crushed in the grip of steel.

'Hooray, mate,' said Ernie, 'pleasure to do business with yer.'

'Yeah,' replied the salesman doubtfully.

CHAPTER SEVENTEEN

With springs squeaking and its tattered canvas roof flapping in the wind, the old bus wheezed and puttered up the main street of Timber Creek. Ernie waved and called out to all and sundry as he drove along. He liked to think he was friends with everyone, but occasionally, his cheery greetings were not appreciated. There was the time he called out to Mrs Dolittle: 'See yer pregnant again, Mrs D. Number five, is it? – and you with the name of Dolittle?' Her husband, Fred, got stuck into Ernie next day at the Golden Nugget and it took all the jokers present to stop Fred from knocking Ernie down. He had apologised and peace was restored once again.

He turned into the parking lot at the pub, right next to his sister's Mini.

'That will make 'er mad,' he chuckled as he switched off to the usual almighty backfire and silence from the dog.

'Sounds like Ernie,' observed Ron.

'Yeah,' chorused the boys.

'I do wish you would call him by his proper name, Ronald,' said Phyllis, who happened to be passing through the bar on her way to a meeting of the Catholic Women's League. 'He was christened Ernest and I don't see why a brother of mine should be referred to as Ernie – it's such an uncouth name. Perhaps if we all made an effort and called him Ernest, he may gain a bit of self-respect.'

'Yes, dear,' sighed Ron. 'But he likes to be called Ernie.'

Ernie charged in the door, colliding with Phyllis as he did so.

'Hi yer, Sis,' he greeted, ''Ow's it goin'?'

'Very well, thank you, Ernest,' said Phyllis frostily. 'I do wish you would get that truck repaired. It lowers the tone of the hotel being parked in the car park. And don't call me Sis.'

'Okay Sis,' replied Ernie. 'But I can't afford to get me truck repaired. Yer see, I've just brought a tractor.'

'What on earth would you want a tractor for?' she asked.

'To get me gear in and out of Pegleg Creek. Yer see the old packhorse was a bloody dead loss. The old bugger was as cunnin' as a double-fleecer ewe.'

'Language, Ernest, language. I will not have you swearing in the bar.'

'I'm not in the bar yet. Soon will be though, if you'll get out of the doorway.'

'Oh,' said Phyllis in an exasperated voice. She swept past her brother, climbed into the Mini and drove off. Laughing to himself, Ernie walked through the door into the bar.

As you can imagine, with Phyllis more or less in charge of things, the bar at the Golden Nugget was pretty well immaculate. She had said to Ron at the outset, 'If I'm going to run a hotel and have a bar, you can rest assured that it will be run properly and it will be kept clean and tidy at all times.' And that was the way it was. The timber top bar was polished until you could see your face in it. The glasses hanging in the racks above the bar were so clean that they reflected the light like diamonds. The carpet was vacuumed each morning and woe betide anyone Phyllis caught flicking cigarette ash on it. The tables and chairs were all new and she said they would be kept that way. In the centre of the room stood a pool table. Phyllis had been against putting one in the bar but, as Ron explained, all hotels had them, and if you wanted the trade you had to have one too. Reluctantly, she had agreed, but told Ron that the games were to be properly supervised and that there was to be no gambling. 'Cripes,' protested Ron, 'The boys only want to have a quiet game.'

'Give us a beer, Ron,' Ernie said. 'In fact, give everybody a beer. I've just bought meself a wee Fergie tractor and I reckon I should crack me whip in celebration, like.'

'Gee, thanks 'Ernest',' joked the boys. 'That's real kind of you, Ernest. We appreciate it, Ernest.'

'Hey, cut out this Ernest thing, will yer,' said Ernie. 'Me sister gets carried away a bit at times, like. Ernie will do nicely, otherwise yer can buy yer own beer.'

That made the blokes shut up pretty quick. Rangi, who had just parked his grader outside while he washed the road dust from his throat, said, 'Hey, what's all this bull about you havin' bought a tractor, Ernie?'

'It's true,' replied Ernie as he reached for his tobacco and papers and rolled himself a smoke. 'A bloke needs somethin' to get his supplies up to The Mansion. And there's me wool to get out.' That was a laugh, too, because there was more wool removed by the blackberry and gorse than was ever taken off by Ernie's shears. He pushed the cigarette into his holder, stuffed it in among the whiskers and lit up.

'Does it go good?' asked Possum Norton.

'Er, buggered if I know,' answered Ernie as he took a long pull at his beer. 'I haven't 'eard it goin'.'

'Aw, Ernie, you're jokin', mate,' said Laurie Scott from the garage.

'Yer didn't buy it without hearin' it run, did yer? Cripes, yer always listen to the motor running before yer buy. Hell, it mightn't even start.'

'Salesman bloke reckoned it was okay,' said Ernie with a hurt look in his eye.

'Ernie, you've got a lot to learn,' said Laurie. 'Bloke was pretty keen to off-load it, was he?'

'Yeah, well, I suppose he was,' replied Ernie. 'But then that often 'appens to me. Salesmen seem glad to see me go. Damned if I know why – I always try and be friendly, like. Anyway,' he continued, brightening up a bit, 'They're deliverin' it to Jock's place in a few days' time.'

'Better get 'em to drop it off at the garage,' said Laurie, who was a kind-hearted man, for a garage proprietor. 'I'll have a look at it for yer. You'll 'ave to pay for any parts, but I'll get the lad to check the timing, clean the points and plugs, and tune 'er up a bit. I'll give 'em a ring when I get home. Where was it you bought it?'

'West Coast Tractors,' replied Ernie. 'Hell, that's mighty kind of yer, mate.'

'Ah, yes,' said Laurie. 'I know the salesman there. Bit of a crafty bastard, that one. I'll tell 'im what'll happen to 'im if he's sold yer a pup. Meanwhile drink up, boys. It's my shout.'

CHAPTER EIGHTEEN

It was a Saturday afternoon and we were all propping up the bar at the Golden Nugget, minding our own business, telling yarns and growling about the government, when the door opened and in walked a stranger. Well, you know what happens when a stranger walks into a bar? Yeah, that's right. They all stare. I guess that's what happened that afternoon. The stranger was a tall, rangy looking joker, wearing jeans and a teeshirt with 'I'M A DINKUM AUSSIE' emblazoned across the front. His jeans were tucked into elastic-sided boots and on his head he wore a khaki slouch hat which covered most of his red hair. His nose was large and hooked and sprouting out from under it was a bushy red moustache. His face was deeply tanned and his eyes squinted as though he had spent a lot of his time out in the bright sun. The thick hair which covered his chest sprouted from the vee in his teeshirt.

He strode confidently up to the bar and said, 'G'day.'

'G'day,' greeted Ron. 'What can I do you for?'

'Gimme a beer, mate,' replied the man as he hoisted himself up on to a bar stool. 'And make sure she's long and cold.'

'Of course it will be long and cold. You don't think I serve beer Pommy-style here do you?' retorted Ron, who had experienced warm Pommy beer when he was in England during the war.

The rangy bloke paid for his beer and emptied the glass in three swallows. He smacked his lips and said, 'Ah, that was good. I'll have another one, please.' Ron pulled another beer and placed it on the bar. The stranger took out tobacco and papers and rolled a smoke. 'Good, beer that,' he said.

'Of course it's good beer!' exclaimed Ron who, being a good Coaster, wouldn't take any criticism of the Coast, its citizens, its climate or its products. 'Brewed just down the road at Port Thompson.'

The rangy bloke looked round the room and, when his eyes rested on us, said, 'G'day, you blokes.'

''Ow yer goin'?' we replied.

He wandered over and had a look at some old photographs on the wall to left of the bar. They were Ron's pride and joy and depicted Timber Creek in the early days. Phyllis used to say that no one was interested in those old things and how much nicer some good paintings would be. Raise the tone of the place, she reckoned. But Ron, who usually lost the argument, was adamant this time and the old photos stayed. Indeed most folk spent some time looking at them.

After examining them at some length the stranger strolled back to the bar and, putting down his empty glass, said, 'I might as well have another.'

Ron refilled the glass and, looking hard at the bloke, said, 'Aussie, are you?'

'Yeah,' replied the man.

'Aw well, we won't hold that against you. Not bad blokes, the Aussies,' said Ron. 'Met a few of 'em in the air force during the war.'

'In the army, meself, mate,' said the Aussie. 'Middle East and then the Pacific when the Japs come into it and we were brought home. Anyway, yer don't happen to know a bloke called Ernie O'Neil, do yer? He saved me life at Alamain and told me he come from Timber Creek. This is the only Timber Creek I can find in Kiwiland.'

'You won't find another one. There's only one Timber Creek. Yeah, we know Ernie O'Neil, don't we boys?' he said, looking at us. 'He should be in anytime. Bit late today but you'll know when he arrives. He drives an old Ford Model A and, if you don't hear it coming, you'll certainly hear him switch it off – sounds like a gun going off. You can't miss it. The whole contraption will blow up one day. His old dog, Rather, sits on the back of the ute and barks all the way from Jock McKenzie's place to the pub. When Ernie switches off, the big bang shuts him up and he lies down and goes to sleep. Mind you, he wakes up pretty quick when Ernie takes him out a pie and a bowl of beer.'

'Jeez,' said the Aussie. 'A bowl of beer! Did you say the dog's name is Rather? Never heard of a dog called Rather before.'

'Yeah, it's true, 'cos Ernie reckons he'd rather be sleeping than workin',' explained Ron. 'He was a pretty good handy dog until Ernie got hold of him. He's spoilt the dog rotten and now he's fat and lazy. Hey, what's this about Ernie saving your life during the war? He's never said anything to us about it, has he, boys?'

'No,' we answered.

'Well,' said the Aussie. 'Give me another beer and I'll tell yer about it.'

Ron refilled the glass and slid it across the bar. The Aussie took a sip and said, 'Maybe I'd better introduce myself. Me name's Andy Miller and I come from Timber Creek in the Northern Territory. It was during the Battle of El Alamain, see. I'd copped a Jerry machine-gun bullet in me leg and fell onto some barbed wire and couldn't get free. Where I was lying was out of sight of the enemy owing to a fold in the ground. It was bloody hot and I couldn't reach my water bottle. I guess I was calling out and kickin' up a bit of a row, like. Anyway, this little Kiwi bloke dashed out of his slit trench and flopped down beside me. He cut me free from the wire, gave me water, bandaged me wound and, when it got dark, helped me back to Allied lines. I gathered, from what his officer said, he was in some sort of trouble but I never saw him again 'cos they shot me into hospital. Never got the chance to thank him properly. It's a long time ago. Stone the crows, it must be gettin' on for thirty years!'

We were all listening to Andy's story with interest and somebody remarked that it was nothing new for Ernie to be in trouble and it seemed, from what he said, that that was where he spent most of his time. Rangi said, 'Better 'ave a beer with us, mate. Fill 'em up, Ron. Don't remember Ernie wearin' any other medals than the ordinary campaign ones at the Anzac Day parades. Hey! that sounds like him now.'

In the distance we could hear the sound of a motor with a serious problem. It rattled, it squeaked and it wheezed. We could hear the sound of it turning into the pub car park, the noise of it almost drowning out the barking of the dog. We heard the scatter of shingle as the brakes were applied and the loud bump as the vehicle met with some immovable object. There was a loud bang and silence from the engine and the dog.

'Wonder what he's collided with this time?' said Ron. 'Hope it's nothing serious or Phyllis will have something to say.'

After a short interval the door opened and in walked Ernie. 'G'day, youse jokers,' he greeted. 'Bit late today, eh? Sorry Ron, hit yer fence but only knocked off a couple o' palin's so it could a been worse. Ha, got a stranger in 'ere 'ave we?'

'Not so much of the stranger, Ernie,' said the Aussie. 'Do yer remember when yer rescued me at Alamain? I'm Andy Miller from Australia.'

'Cripes mate, yer jokin'! exclaimed Ernie. ''Ow did yer find me?'

'Only Timber Creek in New Zealand, Ernie. Anyway, 'ow yer goin', mate?'

Andy stuck out a hand which Ernie grasped with a firm grip. 'Just as well the blokes 'ere were able to identify yer,' continued Andy. 'Wouldn't of known yer with them whiskers.'

'Grew them after I came out of the army,' explained Ernie. ''Ad enough of that shavin' caper to last me a lifetime. Anyway, drink up, you blokes. The beer's on me. What made yer leave Aussie and come over 'ere?'

'Well, yer see, it gets bloody hot and humid up in the Territory in the summer-time and she rains like she's never goin' to stop, so I says, mate, yer'd better get away from this for a while and go over and find old Ernie – so 'ere I am. Wanted to say thanks for savin' me life. It mightn't be a very useful life but it's the only one I've got.'

Ernie and Andy had a lot to talk about so we left them alone and moved down to the other end of the bar, after all, they hadn't seen each other for twenty years.

On being asked why he hadn't received a medal, Ernie explained the situation, 'Bloody lucky I didn't get me self court-martialled' he said. 'Where are yer stayin?'

'In the pub at Port Thompson,' replied Andy. 'I've got a job workin' as a builder's labourer for a few weeks,' said Andy. 'Might stay on over 'ere for a while. I'm sick of the bloody heat and the flies over there. When it's not rainin' the sun fair burns yer up, and when it rains yer wish the sun would shine again. Fair dinkum, mate, it'll rain solid for a fortnight up where I come from. Man's never satisfied, I guess.'

'Rains a lot 'ere,' said Ernie, 'But when she's fine there's nowhere better.'

The two men talked on into the evening. Ron officially closed the bar at six o'clock but, being on the Coast, nobody took much notice of that, and blokes continued to come and go as they liked. Three rings on the doorbell always gained admission. Phyllis, of course, had tried to put the kibosh on the after-hours trading but even she realised that you couldn't change a West Coast tradition and had to back down. Mind you, Ron never heard the end of it. Not that he minded working in the bar in the evenings – it got him away from Phyllis' nagging.

Andy and Ernie had a meat pie each and continued their talking. It was about 11pm when Andy finally went out to his rental car to drive back to the Port.

'Be careful, mate,' warned Ernie. 'That parasite, Traffic Officer Giles, might be out on patrol. Never sleeps, that bastard.'

CHAPTER NINETEEN

It's amazing how blokes like Ernie seem to be able to get on the wrong side of authority. I'm sure many of them don't try to upset the law but somehow it just seems to come naturally to them. I mind the time when Ernie had a run-in with Traffic Officer Giles; the one the boys called Hitler. But I guess he was only trying to do his job and, after all, coming up against Ernie at times would make anyone a little Hitler. Anyway, I've only got Ernie's version of this incident and I've had to try and make sense out of what he told me one day at the Golden Nugget. It all started when he and I arrived out front at the same time. I was amazed to see him step out of a Holden ute.

'Hey, Ernie,' I asked. 'What happened to the old Model A?'

'Come into the pub and 'ave a beer and I'll tell yer,' he replied.

We went into the bar to be greeted by Ron, who was on his own catching up with the news in the morning paper. 'G'day,' he said. 'The usual, boys?'

'Yeah,' we answered.

Ron filled our glasses and we said, 'Cheers,' and removed the top half of the brew.

'Okay Ernie,' I said. 'Spill the beans. You want to listen to this, Ron. Old Ernie's goin' to tell us about a run-in he had with Giles.'

It appears that Ernie was steaming along in the old Model A at his maximum speed of about twenty-five miles per hour. He was heading into Port Thompson to watch the West Coast play Canterbury in a rep match at Rugby Park. About ten kilometres beyond the main road junction, he came round a bend and there was Traffic Officer Giles sitting in his patrol car doing things that traffic officers do – like our Ernie. Concentrating on holding the old bus on the road, Ernie failed to see his enemy and tootled unconcernedly on his way.

Traffic Officer Giles, seeing the truck weaving backwards and forwards across the centre line, started his car, switched on his siren and flashing lights, and set off in pursuit. Owing to the clatter of the clapped-out engine, the flapping of the loose canvas roof and the barking of the dog, Ernie failed to hear the siren and, as he didn't have a rear-vision mirror, he also didn't see the flashing lights. After about a kilometre Giles decided that this called for sterner measures so, speeding up, he drove alongside Ernie and signalled him to pull into the side of the road. Ernie, seeing Giles waving at him, thought what a friendly cop he was and, waving back, continued on his merry way.

Giles was, by this time, getting pretty stroppy. He pulled out in front of Ernie and forced him to stop. Having switched off his engine and put on his cap, he got out of the patrol car and strode back to Ernie's truck, which Ernie had fortunately managed to stop before he ran into the back of the patrol car.

'Good afternoon, sir,' said Giles in his best official voice. 'Why didn't you…'

'Gee mate,' interrupted Ernie. 'That was a bloody stupid thing to do, cuttin' in on a bloke like that. I nearly ran into yer.'

'If you'd stopped when I signalled,' said the officer, 'That wouldn't have been a problem. Have you got a warrant of fitness for this vehicle?'

'Think she might 'ave expired, like,' said Ernie.

Giles looked at the faded old label on the windscreen and said in horror, 'Good God, man, it expired three years ago.'

'Gee!' exclaimed Ernie 'Doesn't time fly. Better get another one, I suppose.'

'The chances of you getting a warrant for this old rust-bucket are about nil,' said Giles, bringing out his notebook and pencil. 'What's your name and do you have a licence to drive?'

'Me name's O'Neil, Officer,' said Ernie. 'And yeah, I've got a licence, but it's at home.'

'O'Neil, eh? Not the infamous Ernie O'Neil from Timber Creek?' asked Giles.

'That's me, Mr Giles,' confessed Ernie.

'All right, O'Neil, I'll give you one week to get a warrant, otherwise I'll order your vehicle off the road. Consider yourself lucky I'm in a good mood today.'

'Okay Officer,' said Ernie. 'I'll take it into Laurie Scott's on Monday. Always does me work for me, does Laurie. Can I go on into Port Thompson to see the footy? Can't get me warrant on a Saturday.'

'Oh, go on then,' said Giles. 'But be warned: if you have an accident your insurance will be invalid, and worse, you'll have me on your back.'

'Old bus isn't insured, anyway,' Ernie said as, with a wave of his hand, he drove on to Port Thompson.

According to Ernie, he got to the game okay. This turned out to be one of the few occasions on which the West Coast defeated Canterbury. Some of the one-eyed Cantabrians had things to say about beer being pumped into their team at a pre-match function, but the Coasters wouldn't go along with that and reckoned it was a clear case of a Canterbury team not being able to have a few beers and play footy the next day and, as the local newspaper said, 'the best team won'. The gallant West Coast team, taking advantage of a wet paddock, had stopped Canterbury from crossing their line and, two minutes from full time, the score was locked at six all… two penalty goals each. Canterbury infringed thirty yards out in front of the posts and the West Coast goal-kicking fullback slammed an easy one between the sticks.

Earlier in the game, during a moment of intense excitement when Ernie was running up and down the sideline, beard split in two and flying over each shoulder, the dog got caught up in the spirit of the game and rushed on to the field. Spying the referee as the only man not dressed in red and black or red and white, the dog immediately attacked him and drove him from the field, much to the amusement of the crowd. The ref took shelter behind the fence in front of the stand until Ernie went over and grabbed the dog. 'The old ref was baled up just like a bloody wild pig in a patch of Manuka!' laughed Ernie. Some of the officials wanted to have Ernie and his dog expelled from the ground but the crowd wouldn't go along with that at all. 'Served the bloody ref right,' they reckoned. 'The one-eyed bastard. Needs a pair of glasses.' So the officials warned Ernie to keep his mutt under control. Ernie dragged a piece of baling twine out of his pocket and tied the dog to the fence. The dog set up a mournful howl and started to chew through the twine. Fortunately the game finished before he got free. Once back on the old truck he was quite happy.

Ernie said that this unexpected win was cause for great celebration that night and large quantities of Coaster XXXX had to be consumed to lubricate throats made hoarse by cheering and giving advice to their team like: 'Get stuck into the bastards' and 'Push 'is face into the mud!'

Ernie apparently couldn't get the Model A started after the party. Whether this was the fault of the truck or Ernie's condition is hard to fathom. Anyway, whatever the cause, he had to be towed back to Timber Creek in the wee small hours of Sunday morning by some of his mates. As the engine wasn't running the dog didn't bark but just curled up on the back and went to sleep. Ernie reckoned this towing caper was pretty good, because you didn't use any petrol and you didn't need a warrant. He wondered if he could get towed more often. 'Like to see the look on Hitler's face,' he said. He left the Model A parked on the forecourt of Laurie's garage and stayed the rest of the night with one of his mates.

On Monday morning Laurie, who lived next door to his garage, got up from the breakfast table, said to his wife, Madge, 'See yer at lunch time, love.' He went out the back door and down the path to the side door of his garage. Selecting a key from the bunch in his hand, he opened the door and, humming a tune to himself, walked through into the workshop and over to the big roller door in the front.

Monday mornings were always something special to Laurie: they meant that he could get back to the work he enjoyed, after the weekend. It was okay in the winter when the rugby was on, but summertime wasn't so good, what with the lawn and garden. He hated gardening but Madge liked everything neat and tidy around the place. One thing though, she didn't object to him going over to the Golden Nugget for a few beers with his mates before tea. Sunday wasn't so bad either: he often took Madge and the kids up to Diamond Lake. He owned a five metre V8-powered jetboat and his eldest, Rebecca, had just learnt to water ski.

He opened the roller door and what met his eyes completely ruined his day. Out front on the forecourt, he saw Ernie's old Model A.

'Oh hell,' he moaned, the song dying on his lips. 'What does he have to leave it here for? And why park it right across the doorway? Bloody thing's clapped out. The little twit will want me to try and fix the blasted thing, I suppose.'

Laurie must have been psychic because, just at that moment, there appeared around the corner a bushy beard followed by a little man who called out, 'G'day Laurie. I've brought me truck in for you to have a look at. Wouldn't start in town after the footie so the boys towed me home. Left 'er 'ere so you could get on to it first thing this mornin'.'

'Ernie,' said Laurie, as patiently as he could under the circumstances. 'I've told you before and I'll tell you again. That truck is stuffed. It's knackered. It's buggered up, down and sideways, and I'm not goin' to have a look at it.'

'Aw gee, Laurie,' said Ernie, completely crestfallen. 'I've gotta 'ave wheels, mate, and Giles says I've gotta get a warrant of fitness or he'll put me car off the road, so could yer give me one of them things too?'

'Ernie,' said Laurie, who by this time was getting thoroughly exasperated – funny how often that happened when folk were trying to get through to Ernie. 'When will yer get it through yer thick skull that I can't do anything with the old wreck? Hang on a minute while I give this guy some petrol.

He went over to one of the pumps, removed the car's fuel cap and, after jamming the nozzle in the tank, went round and washed the windscreen.

'G'day, Ernie,' said the bloke. 'Havin' trouble with the old Model A?'

'Yeah,' replied Ernie. 'Laurie doesn't seem too keen on fixin' it. Reckons it's had it – but that's what he always says.'

The bloke said to Laurie, 'Put that on me account, Laurie. You want to kid Ernie into gettin' a new one.' And, laughing, he climbed into his car and drove away.

'There yer are, Ernie. That's a second opinion for yer. Now will yer believe me? That truck's as stuffed as the big trout on the Golden Nugget mantelpiece.'

'What am I goin' to do?' asked Ernie sadly.

'Tell yer what to do,' Laurie replied, thinking that maybe old Ernie was at long last starting to see reason. 'Why don't yer go round to Paddy Hannon's and see what he'll give yer for it, and I'll ring up me mate Phil Gordon, at Port Thompson Motors. He's the president of the Ford Owner's Club. Maybe one of his members would take it off yer hands for a few bucks. Then yer can sell it to whoever offers the best price. But don't count on gettin' much for the old heap. She's really only worth scrap value.'

'Yeah!' exclaimed Ernie excitedly 'Then I could use the twelve hundred I had over from the purchase of the Fergie. I might even be able to touch Phyllis for a few bucks. She'll be glad to see the back of the Model A. She says it lowers the tone of the pub havin' it parked out the front, whatever that means.'

'Doesn't do a hell of a lot for my garage, either,' muttered Laurie. In a louder voice he continued, 'Yeah, you do that, Ernie. But look 'ere, mate, before yer buy anything let me have a look at it. You know, it's almost more in *my* interest that yer get something reliable than it is in yours'.

''Ow do yer make that out?' asked Ernie with a puzzled frown.

'Yeah, well never mind, mate. You go and see Paddy and I'll give Phil a ring.'

CHAPTER TWENTY

Ernie scuttled down the side-street as fast as his bandy little legs would carry him to Paddy's place. 'Gee,' he said to himself. 'Good bloke, old Laurie. Always ready to help a feller. Great the way he checked over the wee Fergie for me. Course I knew he wouldn't find anything wrong with it. A bloke could tell the salesman was an honest guy. When yer get to my age, yer can tell who's a ratbag and who isn't.'

He reached Paddy's gate, or where the gate would be if it wasn't lying on the ground. Paddy always instructed everyone to shut the gate when they left. I reckon he really believed that the gate was still in place. Ernie rushed through the gap and up the path to the front door, dodging sundry articles of junk on the way. He knocked on the door, opened it and called out, 'Are yer there Paddy? I've got somethin' yer might be interested in.'

'I'm down in the kitchen, so I am. I'm busy stocktakin', boyo,' replied Paddy.

Ernie trotted down the hall and found Paddy standing at the kitchen table, struggling to remove a reluctant bolt out of the back plate of a diffy. He set down his socket wrench and, mopping his brow with a piece of dirty cotton waste, said 'Ah, it's yourself, Ernie. Good day to you. As I said I'm busy stocktaking. Got to get this valuable piece in working order so me books will be in order. And what would you be havin' that would interest an Irishman other than a good fight, a glass of Guinness or an Irish Mist whiskey?'

'It's me old Model A, Paddy. Laurie says he can't fix it any more and Hitler won't let me go on the road without a warrant, so she's for reluctant sale. At a price, that is, of course,' he added with cunning gleam in his eye.

'Ernie,' said Paddy. 'I know that old Model A better than I know when St Patrick's Day is. Many is the time I've supplied you with parts, at a discount price of course, to keep it on the road, so I have. It's only worth scrap value, boyo. A man could only allow you fifty dollars for it – and even then I'm being too generous.'

'Fifty dollars! fifty dollars!' gasped Ernie. 'I'm tellin yer, that old bus is a collector's item. It's vintage, mate. I'm sorry, Paddy, but I'm sad and hurt that someone I looked on as a friend would insult me like this.'

'Please yourself, Ernie,' said Paddy as he picked up his wrench and attacked the bolt again. 'But friend or not, that's my best offer. I've got a business to run, so I have.'

'Okay' said Ernie as he made for the door. 'I'll keep yer in mind when all the offers come in, but don't think yer can beat me down.'

'You'll not forget to shut the gate on the way out, Ernie?' called Paddy.

Back at the garage Ernie found Laurie replacing the receiver on the phone.

'Just been talkin' to Phil,' he reported. 'Apparently Len Black is restoring a Model A and he'll give yer a hundred and fifty for the truck without seein' it. Now that's a hell of a good offer and I'd accept it if I were you, Ernie.'

'Yeah,' said Ernie. 'It's not much but it's more than that miserable old Irish bastard would give me. Fifty dollars, Laurie. Did yer ever hear the like of it? And they reckon the Scots are tight. They wouldn't hold a candle to the Irish.'

'Well, Ernie, that's all beside the point. Shall I ring Phil back and say yes?'

'Okay' replied Ernie. 'I'd better make the sacrifice, I suppose.'

Laurie rang Phil said, 'Yeah, that's okay, Phil, Ernie's going to make the big sacrifice. His words, not mine. Can you arrange with Len for him to come up and collect the Model A?'

Ernie was by this time pretty wound up and he said excitedly, 'That gives me $1850! What do yer reckon I'll get for that, eh?'

'Not a hell of a lot,' said Laurie. 'I reckon yer'd better go and touch yer sister for a few bucks. Yer want to get somethin' that's goin' to be a bit reliable.' He didn't like to point out that anything that Ernie owned wouldn't be reliable for very long.

'Okay. I'll go and see her now,' said Ernie. 'Hope she's in a good mood.'

He hurried across the road to the Golden Nugget and went round to the back door as the bar was not open. Pushing open the door he walked into the kitchen to find Phyllis washing the breakfast dishes.

Just the opposite of Ernie, she was a tall, well-built woman. Rather attractive too, but that attractiveness was often marred by the look of petulance on her face. Ernie reckoned the main trouble with his sister was that she always had to be so bloody correct. He could even imagine her and Ron having sex: it would have to be done so correctly – probably by numbers, chuckled Ernie to himself.

'G'day, Sis,' he greeted her brightly. 'Woman's work never done, eh?'

'Ernest,' Phyllis replied in acid tones. 'How many times must I tell you to knock before you come in? It's embarrassing to Ronald and me to have you barging in like that – and don't call me Sis.'

'Okay Phyllis,' said Ernie, not wanting to upset his sister more than usual. 'Sorry, but Ron said for me not to knock. "Just come straight in, mate, you're part of the family," he said.'

'Oh, did he?' said Phyllis. 'I'll have to have a word with Ronald. And what do you want at this hour of the morning, Ernest? Bit early for you, isn't it?'

'Well, Phyllis,' said Ernie trying to be as diplomatic as possible, not an easy task for our friend. 'You know 'ow yer don't like me old Model A parked outside the pub?'

'Yes,' answered Phyllis cautiously.

'Well, Laurie Scott at the garage says he can't fix it any more and 'e can't give me a warrant. Giles says if I don't get a warrant he'll order the old bus off the road, like.'

'So it should be off the road, Ernest. It's a disgrace to the family. What your father would have thought about it I don't know.'

'Probably not much' pointed out Ernie 'After all, 'e didn't own a car. Reckoned they were extravagant and the work of the devil or some such.'

'Well what's this got to do with me?' asked Phyllis, wishing her brother would get to the point.

'Well, Phyllis, I was wonderin' if you could make a bit of a contribution towards the cost of a new one, like, and then you wouldn't 'ave to worry about me old wreck parked out front.'

Phyllis thought for a moment and then said, 'Sit down at the table, Ernest and I'll make a cup of tea. Then we can discuss this proposition of yours.'

She went over to the bench and plugged in the electric kettle. Ernie sat down on one of the comfortable chairs at the kitchen table and looked round the room. He didn't often get past the bar and into his sister and brother-in-law's private quarters. Since he was last in the kitchen, the whole room had been renovated. Bit poncy, he reckoned as his beady little eyes took in every detail.

The walls and ceiling were painted off-white. The doors were pale green, as were the cupboard doors in the new bench unit. There was a new, sparkling white electric range with matching range hood. Beside the range and under the bench there was a new dishwasher, which Phyllis seldom used as she would never concede that it would wash the dishes as well as the good old-fashioned way. However, 'We must have one, Ronald. Everyone else has one', she had said. The twin sink with the Wastemaster was new, as was the stainless steel bench. The area between the sink and the window-sill was tiled. Expensive looking floral curtains waved in the breeze from the open window which looked out on the surrounding bush-clad hills. On a smart-looking pine wood dresser there was a small TV set, a photograph of Phyllis and Ron on their wedding day, one of their daughter, and a vase of flowers brought in by the Misses Monaghan. The floor was covered in new and obviously expensive vinyl. Been quite a bit of the old foldin' stuff flung around 'ere, said Ernie to himself. Still, I reckon I'm better off in the old shack up Pegleg Creek. Up there yer don't 'ave to worry whether the place is clean and tidy or not and, besides, visitors feel much more at 'ome among the simple things. Not that Ernie was inundated with visitors – most folk steered clear of the place.

I remember the time when Ernie invited us up to his place. It was in April and we were all in the bar at the Golden Nugget having a few beers, when in walked Ernie. Ron poured him his usual brew and he took the top half off the glass, wiped the froth off his beard with the back of his hand, belched and said, 'Bugger the suds.' Then he drank the rest, put the glass back down on the bar and said, 'Whose shout is it?' After Rangi had bought a round, Ernie said, 'Hey youse jokers, there's a couple of stags roarin' up the top end of my place. They come out and challenge each other in the mornin' and evenin'. What about you all comin' up and we'll 'ave a go at 'em. Yer could stay at my place for the night and then we could get at 'em early in the mornin', like.'

Three of us said, 'Yeah, we'll go,' so it was all arranged for that night. The other jokers all declined, having urgent things requiring their attention, even Possum Norton who, when he wasn't trapping opossums, was a real keen man on the deer. These guys all grinned a little and wished us luck, but we didn't take too much notice of that, thinking that there would be all the more venison for us. Of course, later we realised why they weren't keen. They had lived in the district longer than the rest of us and had known Ernie longer.

Anyway, away we went with our rifles and sleeping-bags and a sufficient supply of beer to last us overnight – never do to run out of the old suds. What a hell of a night it turned out to be. What with Ernie's snoring and the attentions of his fleas, we spent the most miserable night any of us could remember. We were all up with the lark next morning and away off up the creek but we never saw a sign of Ernie's deer.

'Cripes!' exclaimed Ernie, 'They've been around for about a week. Wonder what has 'appened to the buggers? Never mind, boys, I'll let yer know when I hear them again and we can 'ave another go.'

By that time we had all made a vow that there wouldn't be a next time: we would be busy like the others. Even digging the garden or painting the house would be preferable to the itch of those flea bites, which we worked on for the next week. The rest of the blokes reckoned it was a bit of a dag.

But let's get back to Phyllis' place and Ernie's quest for financial assistance. She poured two cups of tea and carried them over to the table. She went to the cupboard and produced some biscuits, which she put on a plate and passed to Ernie.

'Gee, thanks Si... I mean Phyllis,' he said as he took a ginger nut and dunked it in his tea. Phyllis eyed this with a frown but Ernie was not perturbed by that and, as the tea was hot, tipped some from his cup into the saucer, blew on it and sipped it noisily. This was more than Phyllis could stand and she turned on him, saying angrily, 'Ernest, there is no need to be uncouth in my kitchen. If that's your best behaviour I think you should leave immediately.'

'Gosh, I'm sorry, Phyllis,' he apologised. 'Guess I'm not used to polite society, as they say. I won't do it any more, I promise.' He hoped he hadn't queered his pitch with his sister as there was nowhere else he could get the money for his truck.

'All right,' said Phyllis severely. 'Now what is this about wanting money for a vehicle? Surely you could get a job and earn some money.'

'Not as easy as that,' Ernie pointed out. 'Yer see, I'd 'ave to 'ave some wheels to get to work. Also, I've gotta come into Timber Creek at the weekends for me supplies and me pension money. (Ernie never called it the dole.) If I 'ad to walk in I'd 'ave to stay the night, like.'

Phyllis had horrible visions of accommodating her brother every weekend; some contribution toward his vehicle might be a small price to pay if it meant that she would be free of him. Just imagine Ernie being in the house when her embroidery circle met on Saturday afternoon. She had plenty of recollections of having him under her roof when he first appeared at Timber Creek after his deer culling down south. Of course, Ronald would think it great to have Ernie around the place again. She just could not understand how her husband could tolerate him.

'Er, how much did you have in mind, Ernest?' she asked, feeling that somehow she was being conned. Mind you, people often got that feeling when dealing with Ernie.

'About a thousand dollars,' said Ernie brightly.

'About a thousand dollars!' screamed Phyllis, who never normally raised her voice. She didn't need to, the tone was usually enough. 'You must be mad,' she continued. 'I would have thought two hundred and fifty would have been extremely generous.'

'Gee,' said Ernie. 'That's too bad. Looks like I will be wantin' to stay 'ere at the weekends after all.'

'Now don't be too hasty, Ernest,' she hurriedly said. 'Maybe I could let you have five hundred – and not a cent more, although what Ronald will say, heaven only knows.'

Ernie chuckled inwardly at this, knowing full well it wouldn't matter what Ronald thought. If Phyllis decided that this was the best course, Ronald would have to go along with it. 'Gosh that's great, S... I mean Phyllis. That should just about give me enough. Yer wouldn't consider the other five hundred as a loan, would yer? No, I can see by the look on yer face yer wouldn't. Anyway, can yer give me a cheque and I'll pay it into me bank account?'

'No, Ernest,' said Phyllis, knowing full well what would happen to a cheque if Ernie got his grubby little hands on it. 'You go and buy your truck then let me know whom to send the cheque to. I suggest you ask Mr Scott, at the garage, to help you in your choice.'

'Yeah, that's okay' said Ernie. 'Laurie has offered to help – 'e says 'e wants to see me with a good set of wheels. Kind bloke, is Laurie. Think I might take 'im up on 'is offer – not that I couldn't pick out somethin' good meself, like.'

'I make that a condition of the five hundred dollars. You must abide by his decision,' stressed Phyllis as she got up from the table. 'Let me know how you get on and where to send the cheque.'

Ernie realised that it was time to go and he got up and said, 'Thanks, Phyllis. Aren't families wonderful? Always there to help each other in a time of need.' He went out the door, leaving his sister a bit puzzled at his parting remark.

CHAPTER TWENTY-ONE

Ernie trotted straight back over to Laurie's garage dashed in the door and called, 'Are yer there, Laurie?'

Laurie slid out from underneath a Holden station-wagon on which he was working. He got to his feet, wiped his hands on a piece of cotton waste and took out his tobacco and papers.

'How did yer get on with yer sister?' he asked.

'Aw, great,' replied Ernie. 'Yer know, she was as keen as mustard about me gettin' a better truck, especially when I pointed out that the old Model A wouldn't be parked outside the Golden Nugget no more. And I told 'er you was goin' to 'elp me get somethin' good. So when does it suit yer to go into Port Thompson with me to 'ave a look round?'

'Now hang on a minute, me old matey. When I said let me look at anything before yer buy it, I didn't mean I was goin' to chase round all the car yards in town with yer.'

'Gee Laurie, I reckon you'd better stretch a point, like. Yer see, one of the terms of Phyllis' gift is that you go with me. Anyway, I was hopin' you'd take me into town, with me havin' no transport. Unless, of course, you can get me old Model A goin' again.'

'No, Ernie. I can't and I won't. That wreck is kaput. All right – be ready at one o'clock and we'll go into town for a look-see.' (Didn't I say that our Ernie was as cunning as double-fleecer ewe?).

At one o'clock Ernie presented himself at Laurie's garage, ready for the foray into the world of truck buying. It was really something for him to be on time, but then this time was really something. It's not every day that a bloke goes out to buy a truck. He had left the dog with Ron at the pub. Ron had secreted the animal down the garden at the back of the shed so that Phyllis wouldn't know that the mutt was on the property. Ron knew that he would be taken to the cleaners if she found that out.

Laurie called out to his assistant, Jimmy, to hold the fort while he was away. He and Ernie climbed into the shop hack. Laurie fired it up, backed out of the workshop and set off down the road to Port Thompson. Ernie was like a kid on his birthday, he was so excited.

'I've got me cheque-book, Laurie,' he said, waving it in the air.

'Yeah,' said Laurie. 'You could give them a deposit with that. I reckon we'll go and see Phil at Port Thompson Motors; he probably won't put one across yer, especially with me being there. But don't get the idea that yer goin' to get somethin' special with the money you've got, and don't think you'll be able to drive it home tonight because they'll want to clear yer cheque first.'

'Nothin' wrong with me cheque,' said Ernie.

'You know that and I know that but those jokers in the car yards don't,' Laurie pointed out. He himself wouldn't have been too keen on accepting one of Ernie's cheques – they'd often been a bit rubbery in the past.

Arriving at Port Thompson, they drove down the main street towards the other end of town, where Phil's yard was situated.

'Hey Laurie, there's the Brian Boru. Let's go in and 'ave a bit of lubrication before we start the business side of things, eh?'

'No way,' said Laurie firmly. 'Business first, personal lubrication later. Besides, I can't be late tonight. Madge wants me to take her out to the pictures.'

A short time later they pulled up outside Phil's car yard. A high wire netting fence enclosed it and streamers of coloured flags, which stretched across the yard, fluttered in the breeze. A small office at the back was the only building on the property. The rest of the area was taken up with a variety of cars and utes in various stages of age and repair.

'Now, Ernie,' instructed Laurie. 'Just let me do the talking. Phil's a good guy but he's also a car dealer and most of those roosters were designed to seperate fellers like you from yer dough.'

Out of the office came a short, fat man wearing a dark blue suit. The shine on the elbows and seat showed that the suit had seen better days. His tie was loose and somewhat askew and he sweated profusely in the northerly wind.

'G'day, gents,' he greeted. 'Looks like rain agin, eh?'

'Yeah, does too,' agreed Laurie. 'Have yer met me mate, Ernie O'Neil?'

'No,' said Phil. ''Ow yer doin' Ernie? Now what can I sell you blokes?'

'Well,' said Laurie. 'Ernie here is lookin' for somethin' to replace the old Model A that Len's buyin'.'

'Got just the thing over here, boys,' said Phil, leading the way over to a nice looking late model Holden ute. 'Low mileage, no rust, really sound condition, radio, heater. Only done fifteen thousand k's. What do yer reckon? Take her for a run.'

'Gee, Phil!' exclaimed Laurie, 'Ernie can't run to a flash job like that, mate. He's only got about $1850 to spend.'

'Aw, right,' said Phil with a disappointed look on his sweaty glistening face. 'Let's see what we've got at about that price. Hang on, there's this 'ere beaut Ford over 'ere at $2400. Not quite as good as the Holden but pretty good considering its age. Good rubber too and new brake linings fitted recently.'

'Gee, I like that one,' said Ernie his eyes fair sparkling. He kicked the front left-hand tyre. He'd seen that done somewhere when someone was looking at a car.

'Now just hold yer horses, Ernie,' warned Laurie. 'There's a lot of rust in them doorsills and round the front guards and yer know what rust is like on the Coast. Eat up a car body like the grass grub will eat up a cow cocky's pasture.'

'Bugger the rust, Laurie,' said Ernie. 'It's the power and the colour that I like.'

'Now look here, Ernie' said Laurie. 'You agreed to let me handle this. In no way are you goin' to buy a bucket of rust 'cos

I'll be the mug that'll have to fix it. Also, yer sister Phyllis would 'ave me guts for garters if I let yer buy something that's no good. All right Phil, what else have yer got?'

'I reckon yer makin' a big mistake turnin' down the Ford,' said Phil. 'But I guess you're the customers.' He thought that this may not be so easy after all. If only Ernie was here on his own, he'd have been able to offload that old Ford, no trouble at all. However, that was one of the problems with being in the car selling game – no one wanted to believe you.

'All right, gents,' he said. 'Yer better come over 'ere and have a look at this Holden. Just come in. Bloke arrived from Canterbury and decided to trade it for a car. Good order at $2200.' They walked over to a red Holden ute which certainly had good bodywork. Laurie had a look at the speedo and said, 'Ninety-eight thousand miles, eh Phil? Is that genuine?'

'Reckon so,' replied Phil. 'Take 'er for a run, eh? Here's the keys.'

'C'mon, Ernie,' said Laurie. 'We'll take her round the block.'

They climbed in, and Laurie stoked up the Holden and drove out on to the street. 'Clutch is a bit sloppy but it only wants adjusting, I reckon,' said Laurie. 'Actually she handles pretty well considering her age. I'd need to adjust the clutch and fit a new set of plugs and points but that's no big deal. The rubber looks good and, as Phil says, there's no sign of rust. Yeah, yer shouldn't go far wrong with this. We should be able to beat him down a bit too. Right, back we go and proceed to do a bit of the old haggling.'

'Yeah,' said Ernie. 'Be just like bein' back in Egypt and bargainin' with the locals.'

'Yeah,' agreed Laurie as he turned back into the yard. 'And just about as tough too, dealin' with a car salesman.'

Laurie pulled up outside the office and switched off the motor. Phil came out of his office, still sweating profusely in spite of having removed his coat.

'Well boys,' he said. 'What do yer reckon? Nice order, eh?'

'Yeah, she's not bad considering the age,' conceded Laurie. 'Wants a few things doin' to it, though. She's really only worth 1800 bucks.'

A look of horror came over Phil's face and he said, 'Aw c'mon Laurie, be real, man. I could probably drop fifty but that's me bedrock.'

'Aw well,' sighed Laurie. 'C'mon Ernie. We'll go round to Mike Appleby's and see what he's got.'

Now, if there's one thing a car salesman doesn't like to see it's folks leaving the yard on their feet rather than behind the wheel of one of his vehicles. Sometimes the supreme sacrifice has to be made.

'Hang on, Laurie,' he said. 'Don't let's be too hasty. Let's say two thousand, eh?'

'Nineteen hundred,' said Laurie.

'Gee, you guys drive a hard bargain,' said Phil 'but, okay, I'll let it go for that. But I'm makin' nothin out of it.'

'Yeah sure,' laughed Laurie. 'My heart bleeds for yer, Phil.'

'But hang on a minute, Laurie,' said Ernie. 'I've only got eighteen hundred and fifty'.

'Yeah I know, mate,' said Laurie. 'But I'll put up the other fifty and you can pay me back – but make bloody sure you do pay me back.'

'Gee thanks Laurie,' said Ernie gratefully. 'Don't worry, I'll pay yer back just as soon as I can. When can I take it 'ome?'

'Phil,' said Laurie. 'Ernie will give yer a cheque for twelve hundred. I'll give yer one for fifty. Now his sister, Phyllis Basset from the Golden Nugget at Timber Creek, is puttin' up five hundred and he's sold his old Model A to Len for one hundred and fifty. That makes nineteen hundred, right?'

'Yeah,' agreed Phil. 'Sounds right to me. Tell yer what I'll do with yer. Give me the two cheques now. I know Mrs Bassett will come across, and I can arrange for Len to pay me: so yer can take it home now, Ernie.'

Well I guess many of you have seen how excited some folk get at the races when their horse comes in and pays a good dividend. If so, then you'll have a fair idea how Ernie behaved. He whipped out his cheque-book, wrote out a cheque for $1200 and thrust it at Phil, saying, 'I'll get away now then, Phil.' He rushed over to the Holden, opened the door, climbed in, and settled behind the wheel.

'Hey, hang on a minute there, mate,' called Phil. 'You've gotta sign the transfer papers before you can go. Keen bugger, isn't he Laurie?'

'Yep,' agreed Laurie. 'When Ernie gets the bit between his teeth there's no holdin' him. C'mon Ernie, we'll go over to the office.'

Ernie reluctantly got out of the cab and followed the other two over to the office. He was a bit hacked off at all this paper-work but supposed it was necessary. Anyway, Laurie would know. When he arrived Phil was sitting behind his desk rummaging in the top drawer. 'Got some transfer papers 'ere somewhere. Geez it's hot, you jokers. Be glad of a few beers after work tonight. Ah 'ere we are. Now, Ernie, just put yer signature there and there and she's all set, mate.' Ernie signed his name and Phil continued, 'All right, me keen old mate. You can take 'er away now and drive carefully for God's sake 'cos she doesn't officially belong to you until the cheques are cleared.'

'You go ahead and I'll follow,' suggested Laurie. 'And, as Phil says, go careful.'

Ernie got back into the truck, started up and with a screech of tyres shot out on to the road, narrowly missing a cyclist as he did so. But the patron saint of cyclists was out on watch that day and the fellow just had a near miss and aged a few years into the bargain. Ernie remarked to himself that it would have served the silly bugger right if he had got knocked over. He weaved his way down High Street, waving to people as he went. Of course, Ernie being Ernie, he failed to stop at the compulsory stop sign at the corner of High and Rimu Streets. This naturally upset sundry motorists, who all decided to test their car horns. Ernie thought how friendly everyone was – admiring his new vehicle, he guessed – so he tooted back and drove on. Laurie, travelling behind, aged about ten years and heaved a sigh of relief when all was well.

Fortunately, that was the only incident on the way to Timber Creek and the rest of the journey passed without further trouble. Well serious trouble, that is. As far as Ernie's driving was concerned, you don't count things like straddling the centre line, failing to signal turns, etc. and, of course, it helped that Traffic Officer Giles was down south that day. Ernie drove up the main street of Timber Creek in great glee. I guess he was smiling right across his face and halfway down his back but, of course, you couldn't really tell because that beard hid it all. He pulled up in front of the Golden Nugget and dashed inside, calling, 'Hey Ron, Sis, come and look at me new wheels!'

CONCLUSION

Well folks, that about wraps up old Ernie for the time being. You see, I have to leave the Coast for a while. Got a big fencing contract up in the Hawkes Bay. Ernie wanted to come with me to 'give yer a 'and, mate,' but fortunately I was able to wriggle out of that one. After hearing about his fencing efforts on Banks Peninsula, who would want him along!

Anyway, when I get back to the Coast again, no doubt Ernie will still be about, so I reckon it won't take long to collect up a few more stories about him. If I can manage that I might just share them with you.

I heard a rumour the other day that he was contemplating going on an island cruise. Yeah, I know, it sounds a bit far-fetched, doesn't it? But then, with Ernie you never know. Anyway, more of that anon.